THE ULTIMATE TEST:

THE LIP GLOSS CHRONICLES

THE ULTIMATE TEST:

THE LIP GLOSS CHRONICLES

SHELIA M. GOSS

Urban Books
1199 Straight Path
West Babylon, NY 11704

ISBN- 13: 978-1-60162-186-3
ISBN- 10: 1-60162-186-8

First Printing June 2009
Printed in the United States of America

10   9   8   7   6   5   4   3   2

Distributed by Kensington Publishing Corp.
Submit Wholesale Orders to:
Kensington Publishing Corp.
C/O Penguin Group (USA) Inc.
Attention: Order Processing
405 Murray Hill Parkway
East Rutherford, NJ 07073-2316
Phone: 1-800-526-0275
Fax: 1-800-227-9604

~ 1 ~

The First Day

Beauty can't be rushed. I've heard that so many times from my self-proclaimed fashion guru mom Destiny Franklin since I was a little girl, so why was she rushing me? "Mom, I'll be downstairs as soon as I find my lip gloss," I yelled over the intercom.

A few seconds later, my mom appeared in my room. "Britney, your face?" She curled her finger towards me. "Come here."

"Mom, hurry up. I don't want to be late on my first day."

"Don't get smart, young lady," Mom said, rubbing off some of the makeup from my face with a tissue.

I listened to her go on and on about the dos and don'ts of wearing makeup. I half-listened as I thought about Jasmine and Sierra, my two best friends since grade school. I wondered what they would be wearing. We always tried to outdo each other when it came to fashion, and today would be no different.

I admired myself in the mirror. My mom stood behind me, admiring her handy work. The makeup applied enhanced my natural beauty. The cherry blossom lip gloss made my lips shiny. My bone-straight jet black hair hung over my shoulders and the two-carat diamond stud earrings my dad gave me just a few days ago sparkled. I looked good in my hip-hugging Baby Phat jeans and pink Baby Phat shirt.

"Get your stuff. Let's get out of here." Mom grabbed her keys and brochures for her monthly meeting with her favorite charity and climbed in the car.

I grabbed my Louis Vuitton book bag and the latest issue of Teen Vogue to look at on the ride over. My mom had what my dad would call a lead foot. She drove so fast that we were pulling up in front of Plano High School before I could get past page ten. We pulled up behind several other luxury cars. "Don't forget I'm going to Sierra's after school," I said.

She responded, "I haven't forgotten. Your dad and I have an early dinner engagement so we'll pick you up on our way home."

My mom and I said our good-byes and I stepped foot on the grounds of Plano High located in Plano, Texas. My legs were a little shaky. I hated to admit it even to myself, but I was a little nervous. I'd heard there were a lot of different cliques so I wasn't sure how me and my girls were going to fit in. When we were in junior high we went to a private school in another part of the Dallas metro area, and everybody wanted to be a part of our clique.

Unfortunately for us, our parents must have had a meeting because all three sets of parents thought going to a public high school would make us so much more rounded. We begged, we pleaded, but since we were all starting our first day of high school here, it's easy to conclude we lost that battle. As I walked to the front of the school building, I didn't see any familiar faces. The girls were looking me up and down like I had something they didn't have. The boys gave me approving nods and I could hear a few of them say, "Dang, she's fine."

I gave them all my million-dollar smile and continued to look for my girls. Sierra was the first one I spotted. She was looking tall and fly with a denim mini skirt and multi-colored top. She had her auburn hair pulled back into a ponytail and was rocking some silver hoops. Her skin always looked tan due to her bi-racial background. She was five foot eight and the tallest out of all of us. I was five six. Jasmine was about an inch shorter than me, but had more spunk than Sierra and I combined.

Sierra saw me and waved. Jasmine turned around and waved too. I didn't immediately recognize her. Jasmine had cut her hair in a bob style. It bounced with plenty of body as we walked towards each other. With or without makeup, Jasmine's mahogany oval face didn't have a blemish on it.

"Hey, girls," I said as we hugged.

"I like those jeans," Jasmine said.

"You can have them after today." I turned around so she could get a good view.

Jasmine rolled her eyes. "Now you know I don't do hand-me-downs."

"That's right, you think you're better than the rest of us," Sierra joked.

"Don't hate. It's enough hating going around," she said as she looked around the school yard.

I shook my head in agreement. "What's up with them?"

"To them we're just token freshmen." Sierra sucked her teeth in disgust.

Jasmine continued, "And they must be jealous."

"So far, I haven't seen any guys that stand out. I mean there are some cute guys here, but you have to have more than a cute face to get my attention."

Sierra and Jasmine turned and said in unison, "Yes, a fine body to go along with it."

I turned around to see who they were talking about. I had to do a double take because the cutest and finest guy I had ever seen was walking our way. I barely noticed the other two guys walking beside him.

"Hi, ladies," the Nubian prince said as he swaggered by us.

"Hi," we all managed to say. I wiggled my fingers in a wave.

He strode by as if he owned the world. While we were drooling over the Nubian prince, I heard someone say, "That's my man, so these chicks need to keep their eyes to themselves."

I'm sure she was doing it for our benefit. I ignored the bad weave on the ghetto-fabulous dressed chick that didn't have a clue about fashion. The last thing we needed was to get in a fight on the first day of school.

Don't let the pretty face fool you. I could get down and dirty with the best of them. My mom was from the ninth ward of New Orleans and my dad was from the third ward of Houston. Although we were wealthy, my parents both made sure I knew how to take care of myself in hostile situations.

Jasmine, on the other hand, was always looking for a good fight. "I know she's not talking to us."

"Chill out, girl," I said.

"It's not even that serious," Sierra added.

Jasmine said loud enough for the girl and her crew to hear, "I'm not scared of anybody."

Jasmine crossed her arms and Ms. Ghetto Fabulous crossed her arms. They were at a standstill. The bell rang to indicate the start of first period. Sierra linked her arm through one of Jasmine's arms and I looped mine through the other and we headed through the doors of Plano High to start our freshman year, ignoring the eyes that penetrated our backs.

~ 2 ~

Teacher's Pet

"Britney Franklin," Mrs. Johnson, my new homeroom teacher, said, pointing to a desk. I hesitantly got up from sitting between Jasmine and Sierra and took my new seat.

She continued to call my new classmates names and they sat down one by one. A cute guy sat next to me, so I didn't feel too bad about being separated from my girls. Besides, we could always pass notes.

Mrs. Johnson continued to call roll. "Jasmine McNeil, you can sit up front near my desk."

I could tell Jasmine wasn't too happy about it from the frown on her face. Mrs. Johnson ignored her. "Sierra Sanchez, you can remain in your seat."

Once we were in our assigned seats, Mrs. Johnson had Jasmine pass out several forms. Mrs. Johnson called on several of us to read aloud some of the rules for her classroom. "Britney, can you read the policy about dress code?"

All eyes were on me. I figured she asked me to read because I was, without a doubt, the best dressed in the class. "Starting next week, all students will be required to wear a uniform." Moans were heard around the class. I continued to read. "If for some reason your parents can't afford to purchase your uniforms, please see your homeroom teacher after class."

I looked at Jasmine and Sierra and I could tell they felt like the rest of the class. We were going to be wearing boring uniforms. There went my plan to out-dress everybody.

"Thank you, Ms. Franklin."

Jasmine raised her hand. The teacher gazed down at her seating chart before acknowledging her. Jasmine said, "Why do we have to wear uniforms? Some of us have bought new wardrobes for the school year."

I heard "yes" all across the room.

Mrs. Johnson cleared her throat and responded, "I would suggest you save those clothes for the weekend."

Jasmine leaned back in her chair and crossed her arms. Mrs. Johnson looked over the rim of her glasses at Jasmine right before writing something down on her sheet of paper. An hour later, we were dismissed to our next class.

We stood out in the hallway and compared schedules. I only had homeroom and geography with Jasmine and Sierra, but we discovered from each other's schedules that we had the same lunch. The rest of the morning went by fast.

At lunch time, we were to meet up outside of the cafeteria. I was waiting on them when I noticed Jasmine and Mr. Nubian Prince walking down the hall together. Jasmine batted her eyes and had the widest grin on her face.

"Jas, I'll see you around," Mr. Nubian Prince said before walking away.

" 'Bye. DJ."

I looked at her. "DJ?"

She was still smiling as if he were standing right there. "Yes. Dylan Johnson, the finest junior in school and he's interested in me."

Before I could ask her more questions about DJ, Sierra walked up in a huff.

Sierra blurted, "I almost got in a fight with the heffa who was talking that smack this morning."

She recanted what happened as we got our food. "Her name is Tanisha Ross and she's a sophomore."

We found an empty table and continued to learn

more about Tanisha from Sierra. "She bumped into me in the hallway and started talking smack. She was like, 'I saw you and your girls looking at my man.'"

"All I know is she better not step to me with that nonsense," Jasmine interrupted.

Sierra continued, "I told her if he was her man then she had nothing to worry about."

"Exactly," I added, adding ketchup to my bland hamburger. I would probably start bringing my lunch, because this food wasn't worth me hurting my stomach over.

"She must not be too smart if she's in my Algebra I class." Sierra used her straw to punch a hole in her chocolate milk carton. "She's a sophomore and you would think she would be in at least Algebra II."

"Not that I'm taking up for her, but you know math isn't one of my strong subjects either," Jasmine stated.

"If there's a sale at the mall, your math is just fine." Sierra spit out some of her milk laughing at my comment.

Tanisha had been declared an archenemy of the Diva Crew. I didn't know her personally, but her attitude toward my friends was enough to make me not like her. "Speaking of Bad Hair Weave, there she goes with her flunkies," I said as she walked by our table, trying hard not to look our way; although I caught her glancing at us on the sly.

We watched them take a seat at the same table across from DJ and his friends. DJ looked our way and for a moment I thought his eyes locked with Sierra's and not Jasmine's. Sierra turned around and looked dazed. Jasmine didn't notice because she was too busy concentrating on DJ. I looked between the two of them. He was cute and fine, but dang, he wasn't all that. I guess I was the only one who wasn't smitten by Mr. Nubian Prince. The guy sitting next to him caught my attention. Our eyes locked. He smiled and I turned away. My girls and I spent the rest of lunch talking about our classes and bemoaning the fact we had to wear uniforms.

"There goes our favorite teacher, Mrs. Johnson," Jasmine said while we walked to put up our trays.

We spoke to her as we passed by. "Ladies," she said, "see you tomorrow. Bright and early,"

As we walked away, I whispered in Jasmine's ear, "Teacher's pet."

She playfully hit me on the arm. "Please. I can already tell she and I will have issues."

"Jas is the teacher's pet," Sierra and I sang as we headed out into the hallway.

The bell rang, ending our singing rant.

"Whatever. I'm going to class," Jasmine said.

We laughed and went our separate ways.

~ 3 ~

One Down, Four to Go

The first day of school was officially over. I couldn't wait to get to Sierra's house to celebrate. Sierra's mom was late picking us up, so we got a chance to stand out front of the school and people watch. Brenda, Jasmine's older sister who was in college, pulled up in her brand new shiny red convertible.

"Hi, girls," Brenda called out the window.

"When I get my license, I know you're going to let me drive," I remarked as I leaned over the door to admire the interior of the car.

"No one drives the Mustang but *moi*." Brenda pulled her sunglasses on and looked in her rearview mirror to reapply some lipstick.

Jasmine's dad, former NFL player Dion McNeil,

owned a few car dealerships. Jasmine knew that as soon as she got her driver's license, she would be able to pick out whatever car she wanted.

"See ya," Jasmine said as she threw her backpack in the back seat and buckled her seatbelt.

Mrs. Sanchez, parked near the curb on the street, attempted to get our attention by waving at us. I didn't blame her for not wanting to get stuck behind the rest of the cars in the circular driveway. "There goes my mom," Sierra said.

We waved good-bye at Jasmine and Brenda, and headed to meet Mrs. Sanchez. "Did you girls have a good first day?" she asked while we buckled our seatbelts.

"Yes, ma'am," I responded.

Sierra seemed excited as she recanted her day to her mom. She left out the part about almost getting into a fight with Tanisha. She saved the issue about the uniform for last. "You have to remember not everybody is as fortunate as you, dear," Mrs. Sanchez said.

"I know Mom, but I had my wardrobe picked out for a whole month," Sierra pouted.

Sierra's birth mom, who was African American, got hit by a drunk driver when Sierra was three. Jorge Sanchez, a prominent Hispanic Dallas real estate developer, married Maria a few years later. She

doted on Sierra as if she were her own child.
Sometimes I think she went overboard. I guess she
was trying to make up for the fact that Sierra lost her
mom. Sierra once told me that Maria was also bi-
racial. She had been calling Maria "Mom" for as long
as she could remember. The only issue between the
two of them concerned Sierra's weight gain from the
summer. Mrs. Sanchez, although not a small woman
herself, seemed to be obsessed at making sure Sierra
trimmed down.

Her dad was very strict and I think that's why their
relationship wasn't as good as it could have been. I
was glad I had a good relationship with my dad.
Maria often refereed the two. If she didn't, Sierra
would be on lockdown and wouldn't be able to go
anywhere. My mom told me that Sierra probably reminded Mr. Sanchez of the wife he lost and he didn't
know how to deal with it. Adults have so many issues.

I pulled out my magazine and Sierra and I took
turns looking at the latest fashions. Traffic was
heavy, so it took us awhile to get to the Sanchez's.
Mrs. Sanchez decided she wanted to lecture us on
the importance of being in high school and not being
caught up with boys.

I wanted to say, "Too late," but I kept my mouth
shut.

"Britney, I spoke with your mom and they may be late picking you up, so you'll be having dinner with us tonight," Mrs. Sanchez stated as we pulled into their four-car garage.

"Can we have stuffed pork chops?" Sierra asked.

Mrs. Sanchez frowned. "We can, but make sure you limit your portion to one."

Sierra looked embarrassed. I couldn't believe Mrs. Sanchez fronted her like that. Trying to pretend as if I hadn't heard the jab, I said, "Come on girl, let's go surf the Net."

I followed Sierra up the stairs. Her room was decorated in everything pink and frilly. Her favorite singer was Chris Brown so she had almost every poster out on the teen sensation. I thought he was cute, but I was more into older men like Marques Houston. *Sister, Sister* is one of my favorite shows and I only watch it because of him.

"Your computer is so slow," I said after trying to log on to a fashion Web site.

Sierra was unusually quiet. She was probably still embarrassed by her mom's comments. I tried my best to cheer her up. "Check this out. Those are the pants you wanted. They're on sale too," I said, rotating the monitor so she could get a better look.

"I have to ask my mom."

"Why? I thought you had your own credit card," I said as we continued to pull up different Web sites.

"My dad said I spent too much money last month, so I have to wait until next month to get my card back."

"That's messed up. Well, I'll get it for you if you really want it. Just promise to buy me something next month." I pulled out my credit card and entered the required information.

"Make sure you have it shipped to your house," Sierra stated.

"Duh. I'm no dummy."

It took me about ten minutes to complete the order. I ordered a cute top covered with butterflies for myself. After placing our order, we tried to log on to MySpace. To Sierra's surprise, her mom had blocked the site, so we turned the computer off and sat on Sierra's bed to talk. We pulled our school schedules out from our backpacks.

"I don't like my science teacher," Sierra commented.

"Mine is all right. He looks a little weird, but he makes the class laugh," I stated.

"I wish I had your teacher. Ms. Houston is boring with a capital B," Sierra said as she closed her bedroom door. She placed her index finger to her lips. "I don't want my mom to overhear."

Must be juicy, I said to myself.

Sierra sat on the end of the bed and asked, "Do you believe in love at first sight?"

"On the soap operas," I responded.

"I think I'm in love."

"Girl, please. You're too young to be in love."

Sierra pouted. "You're sounding like my mom."

I didn't like the mama comparison. "There's not one boy that can make me fall in love," I said with confidence.

"You'll feel that way one day."

"Who is this guy that has your nose wide open?" I asked, although I had a feeling I knew who.

"Dylan. He's so cute and smart and he says he thinks I'm cute." Sierra looked like she was in LaLa Land with a smile plastered on her face.

We spent the rest of the afternoon talking about our first day and counting down to the weekend. Dinner was great and Sierra ate more than one stuffed pork chop. I saw her mom cringe when Sierra took several bites of the second one. It was after eight when my parents came to pick me up. It had been a long day and after taking a bath, I crashed.

My cell phone rang, but by the time I found it to answer, the call had gone to my voicemail. I relaxed across my bed and listened to Jasmine's message.

"Guess who called me. DJ. Can you believe it? He called me already."

I could hear the excitement in her voice. I stared at my phone. *What was with this DJ guy? Don't tell me that my two best friends are falling for the same guy.* I sat straight up in the bed. *Houston, we have a problem.*

~ 4 ~

The Mall

Lil' Mama's song, "My Lip Gloss" blasted from my iPod earpiece as I waited for Jasmine and Sierra in front of the food court at the Galleria. I had been waiting on them for fifteen minutes. Fortunately, I had my music to keep me company or I would be upset. Being on time is a quirk of mine, but Jasmine and Sierra could care less.

"What's up?" Sierra asked from behind me. She slid into the chair opposite mine.

I looked around. "Where's Jas?"

"She called. She's waiting on Brenda to drop her off. They had to make a few stops beforehand."

"I wish I had a car like Brenda."

"Me too. I'm hoping to get one for my sixteenth birthday."

"I want one for my fifteenth," I said. I pulled out my compact mirror and applied some cotton candy lip gloss to my lips. "Jas needs to hurry up. I want to check out the new lip gloss at the Lancome counter."

"Oooh, don't look, but trouble is walking this way."

I slowly put down my compact mirror and my eyes locked with Tanisha's. She rolled her eyes. I rolled mine back. She was by herself. She strolled toward our table. Neither I nor Sierra said a word. She stopped in front of our table and plastered on a fake smile. "Where's your sidekick?"

"If you mean me, I'm right here. What do you want?" Jasmine sashayed around Tanisha, paused, looked her up and down and took a seat next to me.

"High school isn't like junior high. You're no longer the popular girls." Tanisha's eyes never left Jasmine's face.

"Ladies, do you hear someone talking?" Jasmine held up her hand in a "talk to the hand" pose.

"No. I only hear you," I responded.

Tanisha got the point and stormed away.

"The nerve of her," Sierra said.

"She's intimidated or else she wouldn't have come over." I didn't know why Tanisha felt threatened by our presence.

"She's an afterthought, let's go to Saks so we can get free makeovers," Jasmine said.

Two hours later, our faces were made up and my bags were filled with several new lip gloss flavors. By now, my stomach was growling and I felt hungry enough to eat a whole hamburger and fries. I don't know which I enjoyed more: the food, the company, or boy watching. I saw a few guys who caught my attention, but Jasmine and Sierra kept finding something wrong with each one.

"He's nothing like DJ," Sierra was the first to note.

"DJ is fine, but he's not the only fine guy on the planet." Their long rave about DJ irritated me. It's no fun to act goo-goo over a guy if your friends aren't willing to join in.

Jasmine threw her hamburger on her plate. "I can't eat another bite. I'm thinking about becoming a vegetarian."

"I love meat too much, so I'm not going to tell that lie," Sierra stated as she devoured the rest of her burger.

Jasmine pulled out two pamphlets from her purse and handed one to each of us. "Brenda says too much meat isn't good for you. She says they put too much stuff in the meat and that's why we have so many health problems."

"I'm perfectly fine," Sierra said in between bites.

"This is just some stupid propaganda. My parents

eat meat and there's nothing wrong with them," I said.

"You guys don't have to do it. It's just something I'm thinking about."

I handed the brochures back. "Don't expect us to give up meat if you do."

She placed the brochures back in her purse and said, "Don't look now, but the Nubian prince is walking this way."

"Hi ladies," Dylan said.

My two friends acted like they were speechless. Since they were, I said, "Have a seat. We're almost through but you're welcome to join us."

"No, that's okay. I'm here with some friends. Saw you sitting over here and thought I would stop by."

Maybe I had one too many ice cubes in my drink, but it seemed as if he was flirting with me in front of my friends. They were so smitten with him, they didn't notice. "See you in school," I said.

"'Bye ladies." We watched him as he turned and walked in the opposite direction.

As soon as he was out of earshot, Jasmine said, "He made a special trip to say hello."

"Now I wish some of the rest of the boys here looked like him," Sierra added.

"Whatever. I just don't see what the big deal is," I responded as I sipped my drink. My two best friends had these foreign looks on their faces. Dylan had them hoodwinked.

"I think we should do a coin toss," Sierra said.

"For what?" I asked

"To see who gets dibs on DJ of course," Jasmine said.

"You two go right ahead. I'm not participating in a coin toss."

"So you're not interested in DJ at all?" Sierra asked.

I leaned back with crossed arms. "No."

"Then my chances have just gotten better," Jasmine said as she handed me a quarter. "The best out of three. Sierra, you call it."

Sierra responded, "Heads."

I flipped the coin and placed my other hand on top of it. I removed my hand slowly. "One for you, Jasmine."

"Yes," she screamed.

A few mall patrons passing by looked our way. I flipped the coin again. Jasmine said, "Heads."

I showed them both the top of my hand. "Now that's what I'm talking about," Sierra said as she squirmed around in her seat.

"Last one. Your call, Sierra." I flipped the coin for the last time and left my hand over it. We waited on Sierra to respond.

"Tails."

I removed my hand and the coin stood on the tails side. I showed it to them both. "I'm the winner," Sierra yelled.

"I think we should do the best out of five," Jasmine said. She always had been a sore loser.

I handed the quarter back to her. "This is silly. DJ seems to be a free agent, but you two are too blind to see it."

"Do I sense a little jealousy?" Jasmine asked.

I rolled my eyes. "Please. If I wanted DJ I could get him."

Sierra chimed in. "Let's forgo the coin toss. Whoever can get DJ to go to the Sadie Hawkins dance will be the winner."

Jasmine placed her hand over Sierra's. "Deal."

They both looked at me. "I'm not participating in it. You two go right ahead."

"Spoilsport."

"No. I just know disaster when I see it and, trust me, DJ is disaster on two legs."

~ 5 ~

The Service

"Shhh. Before one of our moms turns around and starts popping off," I said to Jasmine as she whispered in my ear about DJ. We were sitting in the pew behind our parents at the Saint John Missionary Baptist Church, where Dr. Anthony Hayes was the pastor.

I hated to admit that on most Sunday mornings, my mom had to drag me out of bed. This morning was no exception. There should be a law about church services starting before noon. Don't get me wrong, I loved my church. We have some of the cutest guys in the Dallas Metroplex attending here. In fact, there was a cutie now who couldn't seem to stop looking in my direction. I glanced in my compact mirror to make sure my lip gloss was popping, and turned and smiled. Between watching the cute guy and listening to Jasmine go on and on about DJ, I don't know what the preacher talked about.

I ignored Jasmine and fantasized about getting to know the cute guy. Jasmine pinched me. It caught me off guard and I yelled out loud. My mom looked back and I waved at her pretending that I was into the sermon. I heard my mom say, "Hallelujah."

I rolled my eyes at Jasmine. You would think with this only being the second week of school, she wouldn't be so caught up in this DJ guy. *I'm tired of hearing about him. What about what's going on with me?* I thought as service ended and we stood in the aisle waiting on our parents to finish talking to other members of the congregation. I looked around for the cute guy, but he was nowhere in sight. *Oh well, I guess I'm stuck listening to Jasmine.*

"What do you think I should wear tomorrow?" Jasmine asked.

I counted on my fingers. "Let's see you can wear khakis, navy blue or hunter green. Not too many choices when you're wearing uniforms."

"Darn it. I keep forgetting."

"Watch your mouth, Jasmine Charlotte," Mrs. McNeil said from behind us.

Jasmine looked my way as if she wanted me to

help her. I shrugged my shoulders. The crowd had thinned by the time we got to the parking lot. Our parents stood outside in the scorching heat and talked some more. I wanted to say, *Do like we do and text message each other later.* It was hot. The dress I wore seemed to be sticking to my body, and I was tired of Jasmine talking about you-know-who. I watched the people go by, and tapped my foot waiting on our parents to end their conversation.

"Britney, come on," my mom said, rescuing me from Jasmine.

"See you later, girl," I said after hugging her.

"I'll text you," she responded.

I hoped not. Jasmine had gotten on my nerves. Sunday's supposed to be relaxing and she had worked my last nerve. We were barely on the freeway when I felt my cell phone vibrate. I removed it from my purse and glanced at the display. It was Jasmine. I turned it off and looked out the window as my parents discussed the sermon from earlier.

The aroma of food hit our senses as soon as we entered the front door. My stomach growled to let me know I was hungry. Our cook, Ms. Pearl, could throw down in the kitchen. I had to get out of that dress first, so I rushed upstairs to change. Less than twenty minutes later, we were all sitting around the table. Sundays were one of the few days we ate to-gether as a family. During the week, it seemed like everybody was on their own schedule.

"Bow your heads," my dad said.

I did, but left one eye open as my mouth watered for the homemade rolls that stared at me. It seemed my dad was praying for everybody in the US and Africa. The food would be cold by the time he finished. He barely got out the "amen" before I reached for the rolls.

"Delicious," I said, savoring every bite. I piled my plate with macaroni and cheese and slices of roast beef. I didn't want any vegetables, but slid some green beans on the plate so I wouldn't have to hear my mom's voice.

My mom and dad both kept looking at each other throughout the course of the meal. At this point I couldn't tell if it was a good or bad thing. I hadn't done anything recently to get lectured on. At least, I didn't think I had.

"How's school?" my father asked between bites.

I was sure he didn't want to hear about Jasmine and Sierra going crazy over this upperclassman, or the fact I hated that we had to wear uniforms when my closet was full of new designer outfits that needed to be seen. No, he didn't want to know the truth, so I answered with a simple, "It's okay."

"Tell me about your classes," he stated.

I love my dad, but his twenty questions annoyed me. Maybe it was his way of trying to bond, I don't know. So as not to hurt his feelings, I told him about each class. I bored myself, but he seemed to be wrapped up in every word.

"I wish gym was the last class because I hate using public stalls," I responded. My stomach was full. Ms. Pearl had outdone herself with this meal.

"Make sure you take some sanitizer with you. I don't want you getting any infections," my mom said.

"Destiny, it's not that bad," my dad responded.

"You don't know what kind of diseases these kids are carrying these days."

I listened to them go on and on about the kids of today. My dad looked strange. My mom stopped talking. Both eyes were on me.

"Dear, there's something we want to tell you," my mom said.

She looked at my dad and he looked at me. "We're expanding."

My mind went blank. *What did that mean?* My mom took over the conversation. Her eyes sparkled. "We're having a baby."

My dad added, "And we wanted you to know that before everyone else."

I opened my mouth to say something, but nothing would come out. I looked at both of them. *How could they do this me? They're old. I'm a teenager.* Talk about a shocker; I was speechless.

~ 6 ~

I Need a Break

Sunday evening went by in a blur. My parents left me to myself so I could digest the bomb they dropped on me. I refused to talk to anyone. The world as I knew it would forever be changed. *How would a little brother or sister affect my life? Would I be required to babysit? I'm in my teen years. This time was supposed to be the best time of my life. Being bogged down with a little brother or sister was not part of the program.* All of this went through my mind as I stood in the girls' bathroom and retrieved my lip gloss from my backpack.

"Oooh, where did you get that?" Sierra asked. She snatched my brand new tube of Grape Delight from my hand before it could reach my lips.

She nearly pushed me out of the way and applied it

to her lips. She smacked her lips together. Normally I would have just let her have the tube, but it had been hard finding it. "Now can I have it back?" I held my hand out, waiting for her to return it.

She passed it to me while admiring the shimmer of glitter on her lips. "Tasty," she said as she licked her lips and tasted the grape flavor.

I threw the lip gloss in my backpack. We went to meet Jasmine at the cafeteria. She stood by the cafeteria entranceway. "What took you guys so long?" she asked.

"Beauty can't be rushed," I responded, in my attempt to get back to my old self. The news of a baby had me out of sync.

We entered the crowded lunch room. The person who I hated to hear about, Mr. DJ, and his crew sat a table in clear view. Sierra and Jasmine pretended to be oblivious and in deep conversation with each other, but walked extra slow. I tapped my foot impatiently. "Ladies, we only have thirty minutes for lunch, so can you please keep the line moving?"

"She's just jealous," Sierra commented.

Oh no she didn't. Please. At least I wasn't being a fool over a guy who was obviously a player.

After we got our tray of food, we searched for a vacant table. Sierra made a detour towards DJ's table. Jasmine frowned. "I don't know why she keeps throwing herself at him. She needs to let him come to her."

I chuckled. Jasmine didn't have a clue about being subtle. She was probably upset that she didn't go to his table first. "Don't hate on her."

"Do it look like I have a reason to hate? Look around." Several guys were looking our way. We found an empty table and took a seat. She went on to say, "I don't have a problem attracting a guy."

"Neither does Sierra."

"I don't want to hurt her feelings, but I think she's too chunky for DJ."

"Jas. How can you say that about our friend?"

"Come on. You and I both know she's been gaining some weight."

"Shhh. Here she comes now," I said.

"I'm just keeping it real."

We turned our heads in Sierra's direction just in time to see her tray of food flying in the air. She did her best to regain her balance but to no avail. I was embarrassed for her. Tanisha said through her laughter, "Sorry, I didn't see you coming."

Jasmine and I pushed past Tanisha to help Sierra to her feet. Fortunately, none of the food had splattered on her. All eyes were on us. DJ did something unexpected. He walked over and helped us pick up what we could, putting it back on the tray.

"I'll get you another lunch," he told Sierra.

"No need to," she responded.

"I insist," he said.

He took the old tray and dumped the food in the trash. Sierra followed us back to our table. I wanted to push Tanisha on the floor for what she did to Sierra. Sierra remained quiet. "I know she did that on purpose," Jasmine said, louder than necessary.

"Drop it," Sierra said, not once looking up.

A few minutes later, DJ arrived back at our table carrying a tray of fresh food. He placed it in front of Sierra. "Thanks, but I'm not really hungry," she said.

"You have to eat something. You don't want my money to go to waste do you?" he responded, getting her to smile before walking back to his table. Sierra's embarrassing situation turned out just fine. I looked into Tanisha's frowned-up face. Her little trick only drew DJ closer to us. Too bad both of my friends were vying for his attention though.

Turning my head around to face my girls, I needed to vent about my own situation. Maybe it would also take Sierra's mind off her little mishap. "I need to tell y'all something."

Sierra stopped playing with her food and looked up. Jasmine barely eats anyway, so I had her attention immediately. I blurted out, "My mom's having a baby."

"A what?" Jasmine asked.

"Wow, how do you feel about that?"

"How do you think? I'm in my prime. I don't have time to babysit."

"That's a little selfish, don't you think?" Jasmine asked.

"I know you didn't, Ms. 'This is my world and you need to get in where you fit in'," I said, snapping my fingers.

Jasmine twirled her straw. "I'm just saying. You should be happy. Now you're not the only child."

"That's just it. I enjoyed being the only child. I got perks being the only child. Now this. My world will never be the same," I said, feeling depressed the more and more I thought about it.

~ 7 ~

Monday Blues

"I expect everyone to dress out and participate in all the activities unless you have a doctor's excuse," my physical education teacher said, before escorting us to the locker room.

Ten minutes later, we were all dressed in our gym shorts and shirts. A few upperclassmen teased us as we walked into the gym. Our teacher had us stretching before starting us in a long workout. Oddly enough, I felt like someone was watching me. I looked up to see one of the guys I had seen earlier with DJ. He wasn't bad looking at all. In fact, he was cuter than DJ. I smiled. He smiled back. I continued to follow my teacher's instructions.

I hated using public bathrooms, and public shower stalls were no exception. I didn't like being sweaty either, so I had no choice but to use the showers in the locker room. Some of the girls in my class got quiet when I walked by. Being in high school could really damage your self-esteem if you let it. The other kids made you feel self-conscious about everything.

It didn't take me long to shower and dress. While packing up my gear, the bell for my next class rang. The guy from earlier stood outside the gym door. "I hope you don't mind. I wanted to wait for you," he said.

"Hi," was all I managed to say as I stood still.

He extended his hand. "I'm Marcus Johnson."

I moved my books around to shake his hand. "Britney Franklin." My heart rate increased as our hands touched.

"Where's your next class?"

"I'm in Mr. Jeter's science class."

"I had him last year."

We began walking toward my next class. "How are his tests?" We were scheduled to have our first test next week and I wasn't sure what to expect.

"His tests come directly from his lectures. Study those and you should ace them."

"Cool, thanks for the tip." It didn't take long for us to reach my destination. I didn't want to be tardy and didn't know what else to say, so I said, "Thanks. I guess I'll be seeing you around."

"Later," he said, before heading in the opposite direction.

I walked into class with a big old grin on my face. Instead of taking notes, I daydreamed about the brown-skinned cutie with short, black wavy hair named Marcus, and doodled his name in my notebook. The cologne he wore had me wondering what it was. I made a mental note to find out what the fragrance was on my next trip to the mall.

"Britney, would you like to share with the class your theory on evolution?" Mr. Jeter asked.

Busted. I stuttered, "According to our book, humans come from apes, but the King James Bible clearly outlines that our heritage started with the creation of Adam and Eve." That was something my pastor had taught us during a youth retreat. I wasn't sure if it was the answer the teacher was looking for, but it was the best answer I had concerning evolution.

"Thank you, Ms. Franklin. I'll take it from there."

A few snickers could be heard throughout the room. I wanted to slide under my desk. This was my last class and I couldn't wait for the day to end. It had been one long day and I couldn't wait to end the Monday blues.

He continued to lecture on the science theory of evolution. This time I paid attention and took notes so I would be able to answer the test questions. The last bell rang. I gathered up my stuff. I didn't want to keep my mom waiting too long; although I dreaded talking about the baby.

"Ms. Franklin, let me see you for a quick second," Mr. Jeter said as students started walking out the room.

He sat on the corner of his desk. "You seem to be a bright student, but today for some reason your attention seemed to be elsewhere. Is there anything going on that you need to talk to someone about?"

"I do have a lot on my mind. But it's nothing really."

"If there's anything and I do mean anything, feel free to talk to me or one of the counselors," he commented.

"Everything's fine. I promise."

"I'll let you go so you won't miss your ride."

Oh no. Now my semi-cute in a nerdy sort of way science teacher thinks I am crazy. I had to be more careful. This was more embarrassing than Sierra tripping in the cafeteria. I rushed to find Sierra and Jasmine before going to locate my mom.

Neither could be found. I turned around and accidentally bumped into Marcus. "Sorry," I said.

"I should have been watching where I was going."

"My mom's waiting or I would stop and talk."

"See you around," he said, not once taking his eyes off me.

I could feel his eyes on me as I located my mom. I threw my backpack in the back seat and turned around. He waved at me. I waved back.

"Who was that?" my mom asked.

"Just a guy I met in gym class," I responded.

"He's sort of cute."

"Yes. He looks all right." This was not the conversation I wanted to be having with my mom. I guess she felt guilty about the baby. I'm surprised she wasn't lecturing me about the dangers of getting involved with a guy at my age.

"Cute or not, be careful. You're too young."

It looked like I spoke too soon. "Mom, you don't have to worry about it. Marcus is cool and all that, but I'm trying to get into Spellman and neither he nor anyone else will distract me."

"If he's going to be your boyfriend, I need to meet him. Know something about his parents."

"He's not my boyfriend," I responded. We just officially met and already my mom had him as my boyfriend. *Hmmm. Marcus and me.* It sounded good to me.

~ 8 ~

The Convo

I could not close my eyes Monday night without Marcus invading my dreams. One dream seemed so vivid. I had just applied some cherry blossom lip gloss and after puckering my lips Marcus leaned to kiss me. That's when a buzzing noise pulled me out of my sleep.

The alarm clock beeped until I hit the snooze button. All I needed was a few more seconds and I would have experienced my first kiss, real or not; I hated that the alarm interrupted me. My eyes barely opened as I went through the motions of getting ready for school. The warm, soothing water hitting my body in the shower perked me up.

"Britney, hurry up," my mom yelled over the intercom set up throughout our spacious house.

I hated rushing. "I'm putting on my lip gloss now," I said after pushing the button.

My dad ate at the kitchen table. "Good morning," I said as I leaned and kissed him on the cheek.

"How's my favorite girl?"

"Fine." I picked up a bagel and spread strawberry cream cheese on it.

"Hurry up. I have some errands to run this morning." My mom stood in the background, patting her foot.

"Have a good day," my dad said as he raised his cup in the air.

I grabbed a few napkins, my bagel, and my backpack, and followed my mom to the car. "Jasmine called for you last night," my mom said. "She said she tried reaching you on your private line but you never answered."

"I was tired. After doing my homework, I went straight to bed," I lied.

"You must have slept too much because it sure took you a long time to get ready this morning."

"I didn't sleep too good," I admitted.

"I've been meaning to ask you, how are you about the baby?"

Should I tell her the truth or tell her what she wants to hear? "It doesn't matter how I feel about it. It's a done deal."

"Yes, it does. We didn't plan for this to happen."

"If you have sex it's a possibility," I responded.

My mom slammed on her breaks. Good thing I had my seatbelt on or else I might have flown out the window. I looked up to see that the car in front of us had stopped. Whew. I thought she was upset at what I said.

"What are they teaching you in school?"

"I learned that two years ago."

"Looks like you, me, and your dad need to have a talk about the birds and the bees."

"Mom, that is so old school. I know how babies are formed. You and Dad did it. You didn't use protection and now I'm going to be saddled with a little brother or sister."

"It's not going to be as bad as you make it seem."

"Can you see it from my view? I've been the only child for how long?" I could imagine her doing the math in her head. I continued to say, "Exactly. So I'm entitled to feel the way I do."

"Look here, Missy. I want your opinion, but what your father and I do is our business. I thought you would be happy. If it had been up to me, I would have had a baby a few years after you were born; but it wasn't."

"Why didn't you try?" I asked.

"We tried and we tried but I could never get pregnant. How do you think I felt when I learned a few weeks ago that I was pregnant? I was just as surprised as you were," she confessed.

"Really?"

"Your father and I look at this as a blessing, and we want you to share in this blessing. We had given up hope of ever having another child."

I felt like they weren't happy with me, as if having me wasn't enough. I didn't like feeling that way. "I'm happy for you and Dad, but what about me?"

"I'm trying to be understanding to how you're feeling, but dear, you have to understand this isn't just about you."

I felt ashamed. *Am I being selfish? Why can't she see things from my point of view?*

As I stared out the window my mom continued, "This new baby will not affect how we feel about you dear. You're my little diva and always will be."

"But Dad," I said, not meaning to say it aloud.

She reached over and squeezed my hand. "You'll always be Daddy's girl. You're the apple of his eye and this baby is not going to change that."

"I'll try to understand, Mom. That's all I can promise."

She squeezed my hand harder. "That's all I'm asking. This is going to be an adjustment for all of us. But together, we'll make it through."

By now, she had pulled up in the school's driveway. The look on my mom's face softened my stance. "I love you, Mom. I'll be all right. Promise."

"Love you too, baby girl." She blew me kisses as I exited the car.

~ 9 ~

A New Attitude

My mind was on my mom and the baby as I walked to the front door of the school. I didn't notice Marcus or DJ and the rest of their friends standing off to the side of the building until I heard someone call my name. I looked up and saw Marcus waving.

I waved back. He left his friends and walked me to my first-period class. "Would you like to sit with me at lunch?" he asked.

"I usually sit with my friends." The sparkle in his hazel eyes dimmed. I added, "But you can walk me to class afterwards if you like."

"That'll work."

We stood in silence as other students walked passed us. "Thanks for walking me to class," I said.

The palms of my hands were sweaty. I avoided wiping them on my navy blue skirt. Something about Marcus made me lose my cool.

"See you at lunch. I better go before I'm late."

" 'Bye," I said, twirling right into Sierra.

Sierra and Jasmine both had frowns on their faces. "What's up?" I asked.

"We waited outside for five," Sierra said.

Jasmine interrupted, "Ten minutes."

Not liking either one of their attitudes, I responded, "As you can see I was in here." I didn't wait for them to respond. I left them standing outside our homeroom class, took my seat, and kept my head down. I avoided looking at either of them.

After class, I lagged around hoping they would both be on their way to their next class. No such luck. "What's your problem?" Sierra asked.

"Nothing. I'll see y'all at lunch." Now they wanted to act concerned. For the last few weeks the conversations we had were all about them. With the new baby and Marcus I needed someone to listen to me, but right now I wasn't in the mood to talk.

The first part of the day flew by. I aced my pop quiz so I was in a better mood when I met Sierra and Jasmine for lunch. Marcus sat with DJ and their friends. He waved at me and I waved back. For some reason DJ thought I was waving at him so he waved.

Although he got some brownie points for helping Sierra, he still was a dog as far as I was concerned.

"I know you're not waving at my man," Jasmine said.

"Your man. He's still on the market as far as I can tell," Sierra stated.

"The Sadie Hawkins dance is a few weeks away so you best be finding you a new date."

"If you're so confident about him, go over and ask him now." Sierra leaned back in her chair and crossed her arms.

"I don't want to embarrass you twice in one week."

Sierra's face turned red. "Chicken." She started making chicken noises.

Jasmine pretended to ignore her. She turned toward me. "What's going on with you?"

Marcus walked over to us. "Hello ladies." They spoke. He focused his attention on me. "You ready?" he asked.

"Sure. Let me empty my tray."

"I got it." He took my tray and went to empty it.

"Who is he?" Jasmine asked.

"I'll tell you later," I said, rushing from the table before they could ask any other questions.

I met Marcus near the front of the cafeteria door. "So how long you all been friends?" he asked as we walked toward my next class.

"It seems like forever, but since grade school."

"I see they got a thing for my boy."

"I guess." If he was looking for confirmation so he could run back and tell DJ, he wouldn't get it from me.

He stopped in the middle of the hallway. "You ain't got a thing for DJ too, do you?"

"If I did, I wouldn't be walking down the hall with you now, would I?" I started walking again. He had to pick up his pace to keep up with me.

"Sorry about that."

I kept on walking. He continued, "I had to ask. You'd be surprised at how many girls try to get to my cousin through me."

I stopped this time. "Cousin? You. DJ?"

"Yes, his dad and my dad are brothers."

Duh. DJ and MJ. They both had the same last name. I don't know why I didn't recognize it before. In my opinion, Marcus was cuter. The only thing Dylan had on him was that he had a wider chest. Give Marcus another year and he could knock Dylan out the box. Lucky for me, Dylan seemed to be the center of attention with a lot of the girls; which meant hopefully I wouldn't have to worry about too many coming after Marcus.

"Thanks for walking me to class."

He pulled his cell phone out from his pocket and turned it on. "What's your number?"

He handed me the phone. I entered my number and handed it back to him. Our hands touched, and it was as if time stood still. The bell broke our trance. He went his way and I went to class.

~ 10 ~

Hey Mr. DJ

Sierra and Jasmine were waiting for me outside of my last class when the last bell rang. They made sure one was standing on either side of me. "I better hurry. I don't want to keep my mom waiting," I said as I walked. They were fast on my heels.

"Britney, who was that guy? Spill the dirt now," Jasmine said.

I stopped. "His name is Marcus. Isn't he just the cutest thing you've ever seen?" I started walking again.

"He's all right. He's no DJ, but I can see why you're starry-eyed," Sierra commented.

Jasmine added, "And you must be careful. He might be one of those guys who try to take advantage of freshmen."

I tuned them out as they gave their opinions on guys. Of course it went back to DJ. If they would have let me talk, I would have told them that Marcus was DJ's cousin, but since they didn't, I kept the information to myself.

I spotted my mom in her silver Jaguar as soon as we exited the front door of the school. "Got to go," I said without waiting for a response. Doggone it. Our friendship was supposed to be two ways and lately I'd been getting the short end of the stick.

I guess they were mad at me because neither one of them called me; nor did Marcus. I was more disappointed about Marcus not calling. *If my friends keep acting like this, I'll have to find me a new set of friends.* What was I saying? Stress was getting to me. This baby wasn't here yet and it already had me stressing out. I vowed to get rid of my negative feelings.

I avoided the topic of Marcus the next day; although I did wonder why he didn't call. Jasmine, Sierra, and I were talking about our homeroom teacher when DJ walked near us and tapped me on the shoulder.

"Marcus wanted me to give you this." He handed me a small white envelope.

"Thanks." I responded.

"See y'all later," he said.

"You can breathe now," I jokingly said to my girls.

Both Sierra and Jasmine let out a huge sigh. I wanted to read the letter but I wanted some privacy. Before I could decide on what to do with it, Jasmine snatched the letter from my hand. I reached for it, but Sierra took it away from her.

"Excuse y'all, but I don't see either one of your names on it." I jerked the letter away from Sierra and threw it in my backpack. "Now nobody will know what it says," I said.

"So DJ and Marcus must be good friends for him to be passing notes?" I knew Jasmine was fishing for information.

"They're cousins," I blurted. I left them both outside the school to ponder that bit of information.

I sat at my desk and read my letter as I waited for the teacher to come in. Sierra and Jasmine kept trying to get my attention, but I ignored them. Marcus had the flu and that's why he hadn't called me. I was glad he at least wrote me a letter because otherwise, I would have put him in the same category as DJ. In between taking notes, I wrote a note to Marcus.

After class, I saw DJ standing near some lockers. I walked up to him and the girl who was standing next to him rolled her eyes. I rolled mine back. "Hey DJ.

Can you give this to Marcus for me?" I handed him the letter.

"Sure. I'll see him tomorrow so I'll give it to him then."

"Thanks," I responded. I moved passed the small crowd.

Jasmine and Sierra rushed up to me. Jasmine said, "You sure you're not trying to push up on DJ?"

"Read my lips." I started to speak slowly. "I'm only interested in m-a-r-c-u-s. Let's say it together."

Since they pissed me off, I said, "You better move up your plans with DJ because some other girl is all in his face. You know the one with the big ghetto booty."

Both of their heads turned so quick, it made me laugh. "I don't know what he sees in her," Sierra commented.

"I know. If he wanted a big booty, he could have you," Jasmine said.

"Excuse me."

"You heard me. If he wanted a big booty." Jasmine used her hand to outline what she considered big. "He could have you."

"You're just jealous because you don't have all of this," Sierra said before slapping herself on the butt.

"Come on you two. DJ isn't worth it."

"Somebody needs to lay off the potato chips."

Jasmine looked Sierra up and down and walked away.

"Jealousy is an ugly color on you," Sierra said loud enough for Jasmine to hear. Jasmine turned around and stuck out her tongue. They both could be so childish.

~ 11 ~

Friday Night Lights

Sierra and Jasmine must have made up because later on that night, Brenda, Jasmine's sister, dropped them off at my house. I was listening to Usher's latest CD, bopping my head up and down, when they walked through my door with overnight bags.

"Ladies, Ms. Pearl made some finger food and left it in the fridge," my mom said.

With everything going on I forgot we had planned a sleepover. We usually had a sleepover once a month. This was my month to host. Thank goodness my mom remembered. I sat up, removed my earpiece, and made room for them on my bed. Jasmine's cell phone rang. She held up one finger for quiet. We made silly faces trying to make her laugh. She walked to the other side of my room and turned her back to us. "So what's up?" I asked Sierra.

She pulled out a flyer from her purse. My eyes got wider as I read the announcement about the dance team's upcoming dance tryouts. "So are you trying out?" I asked.

"I'm thinking about it."

I hooked my iPod up to a speaker and clicked to find Usher's latest dance tune. Sierra and I started dancing. Jasmine ended her phone call and sat on the bed. "You two look silly."

"You're just mad because you're the only black girl I know without rhythm," Sierra said.

"I have other skills. Besides, I want to be a cheerleader. I'll leave the dancing to you two," Jasmine responded.

"Ladies. No fighting. This is Friday night. We don't have school tomorrow. So party," I said as I turned up the volume on the speaker. I grabbed Jasmine by the hand and pulled her up. "See, all you have to do is move to the side and glide."

She bumped into me and then Sierra. We danced until we all got tired, falling out on the bed. "I'll cheer you on from the sidelines, but I won't be trying out for dance. I want to be a cheerleader, so I'll save my energy for that."

"You can't try out for cheerleader until next year," I responded.

"That's cool. I can wait until then. I'm bored," Jasmine said as she flipped through one of my magazines.

I turned on the computer. "Let's see whose on MySpace," I suggested. After bypassing the firewalls, I logged on. Jasmine and Sierra pulled up chairs and sat next to me as we surfed pages and left comments on some of our friends' pages from our old school. "I wonder if DJ has a page," Sierra said.

I used the search option and put in various versions of his name, but nothing came up. "Someone's got a secret admirer," Jasmine noted.

I clicked on the message and my computer started acting crazy. "It's spam. Darn it. It must be a virus." I tapped several keys on the keyboard until the screen stopped moving. "Now I got to run the virus scan." I clicked on the virus scan icon. "It'll take all night to run." I turned off the computer monitor.

"So what now?" Sierra asked.

"Bri can tell us about Marcus," Jasmine said, as I turned to face them.

I crossed my legs and looked out into space as I thought about Marcus. "There's nothing to tell. He's walked me to class a few times. That's about it."

"What was in the letter?" Jasmine asked.

I got up and retrieved the letter from my diary. I handed it to them. "See? It was nothing."

Sierra stood over Jasmine's shoulder as they read it together. "Looks like you've been holding out. What if he asks you to be his girlfriend?" Sierra asked.

"I'll have to think about it. He's the first boy I've really found interesting. Most of the other dudes seem so into themselves."

"He's no DJ, but he is cute," Jasmine stated.

I pretended she didn't make a wisecrack about Marcus. "I need to say something and I hope neither one of you take this the wrong way." I looked at them both before continuing. "This thing with DJ is getting out of hand. It's obvious he's a player."

Jasmine leaned back and crossed her arms. "You forgot about Brenda. She's taught me everything I know about guys."

"But you said she can't seem to keep one guy," I said.

"That's by choice. She says if a man starts tripping, kick them to the side and find another one."

"If that's the case, why are you competing with one of your best friends, when you can easily find some other guy to go with to the Sadie Hawkins dance?" Jasmine was jealous of Sierra. She knew it. I knew it, but she would never admit it.

She stuttered. "Because. It's not like either one of us *really* like him."

"Speak for yourself," Sierra responded.

"Come on now. We just met this dude. I only want him because he seems to be popular."

"Back off. I think he's more than just a cute face. He showed me that when he helped me when Tanisha tried to trip me that day in the cafeteria."

"Girl, be for real. He was just feeling sorry for you."

"Enough," I yelled. This was going to be a long night.

"I'm just saying," Jasmine said. "You shouldn't be catching feelings for a guy who obviously has a lot of girls after him."

"You're one to talk Jas. You're one of those girls," Sierra responded.

"I told you my purpose. If it works out, fine. If it doesn't, my world isn't destroyed."

"Then as your friend, if I tell you that I'm interested in a guy, you should back off."

"Not if I know the guy will only hurt my friend."

They went back and forth and I sat on the sidelines observing. The bickering got on my nerves. "Why don't you both just forget DJ and problem solved," I suggested.

"It's not going to happen," Sierra stated.

"I'm only trying to spare your feelings. Let's face it. Why would he go after you when he can have this."

I wanted to slap Jasmine myself. Lately, she had been making comments about Sierra's weight. I'm sure Sierra knew she had gained some weight, but she was nowhere near fat. I didn't know why Jasmine and Mrs. Sanchez wanted to allude to her weight all the time. Well, to me it seemed like they did it more than they should. Sierra never responded; instead she left the room. "You can be so cruel sometimes, Jas," I said, as I left the room in search of Sierra.

I found her downstairs looking out the patio door. "You know she's right. Why would he want me?"

"Sierra, Jas is just tripping. Don't listen to her."

Behind us, Jasmine said, "Yes. Don't listen to me. I'm sorry."

For now at least, all was well in our world again. But I had a feeling this was the beginning of the end. Our friendship would never be the same; however, I hoped I was wrong.

~ 12 ~

Dancing Machine

"One . . . two . . . one . . . two . . . three," Jasmine yelled out as she coached Sierra and me. We were in a vacant class room practicing for the dance tryouts that were in less than thirty minutes.

"Okay ladies, you'll do fine."

"I wish we would have had more than a weekend to prepare," I said as I wiped the sweat from my forehead with a pink towel.

Sierra drank some vitamin water and did a few stretches. She threw her towel in her bag. "Let's do this."

We high-fived each other and walked to the gym with confidence. "Don't look now, but guess who's coming this way," Jasmine said.

DJ and Marcus were walking in our direction. I didn't know Marcus was back in school because I hadn't seen him all day. From the stride in his step, it was hard to tell he had recently had the flu. "Ladies, I heard you were trying out," DJ said as he stood between Jasmine and Sierra.

"On our way there now," I said without taking my eyes off Marcus.

"Can I talk to you for a minute?" he asked.

Jasmine looked at her watch. I knew I didn't have much time, but I did want to talk to Marcus in private. "You all go ahead. I'll be there in a minute."

DJ walked with them toward the gym. Marcus and I lingered behind. "You look good."

"You look good too." And oh, did he look good. He had changed out of his school uniform and rocked a Nike jogging suit with what looked like the latest pair of Air Jordans that matched. His cologne had me swooning.

"So what song are you dancing to?" he asked.

"One of Ciara's old songs."

"I sure wish I could watch. The coach says the gym is off limits until after the dance tryouts."

Fortunately for me, he wouldn't be there to watch. I was nervous enough. I didn't need him looking on or else I knew I wouldn't be able to remember the routine I'd rehearsed. We were not that far from the gym. DJ held the gym door open as other girls went through.

"I guess I better get going."

"I'll call you tonight."

"I'm so nervous. I might be crying on the phone."

"You'll do fine. If you dance like you walk, you already got it."

My cheeks flushed. Jasmine walked out the door. "Come on girl, or you can kiss this audition good-bye." She grabbed my arm and pulled me towards the door. "Talk to you later, Marcus," I said.

I didn't expect to see so many girls. The benches were full. It appeared, we would be here a long time. I signed in as instructed, placed the number on my shirt and took a seat next to Sierra and Jasmine.

"Oh no. Not Tanisha and the heifer crew," Sierra said as I followed her gaze.

Tanisha said, "Ladies, you can go home now, because we got the available spots."

We ignored them as they passed us and went up a few benches. I didn't feel comfortable knowing she was sitting above and behind me. *If I feel anything slimy on me, I will personally get up and kick her butt.* A petite brunette woman carrying a steno pad and pen spoke into a microphone and stood in front of our benches. "Ladies, I need to have everyone's attention. I'm Ms. Albright." She went over the rules and expectations. "We normally break up the auditions into two parts, but we're on a time crunch. You will do your own routine and you'll have fifteen minutes to learn a new one."

A girl dressed in a shorts set trimmed in silver glitter walked to the front. "I'm Nikki and I'm the dance squad leader. I'm a senior so this will be my last year. It's my job to make sure everyone on the team knows the routine. We only have a few slots, so ladies, give it your best shot and may the best girl win."

The crowd cheered. I felt hyped. I pulled out the CD with my music on it. Ms. Albright broke us up in teams. Sierra and I were on the same team. "I don't know if I can do this," Sierra said between clenched teeth.

I whispered, "Oh, you're going to do this."

Her makeup dripped from her face. I handed her a clean towel from my bag. "What if they choose a song that I can't dance to?"

I was supposed to be the nervous one. We always teased Sierra of being a cross between J-Lo with the big booty and Janet with the dance moves. She was not going to freak out on me now. I wasn't going to let it happen. "Take a few deep breaths. Don't make me have to slap you straight."

She laughed. It seemed to ease the tension. We followed the instructions given to us. We each took turns doing our dance routine. When it came to my turn, I felt confident in my abilities. I pretended as if I were at home in front of my floor-length mirror doing my thing. As soon as the music blasted from the speakers, I became a dancing machine.

The smile on the judges' faces inspired me to keep doing my thing as my body felt in sync with the music. When my routine was over, I took my seat next to Jasmine and she whispered in my ear that she thought I did well. Sierra was up next. She added a few extra moves we hadn't rehearsed. If she didn't make it, I would know the judges were on the take. After she finished, I went back to the floor to do our group dance.

Brenda waited for us outside. "So did y'all make it?" she asked as we got in her car. I was glad to be getting the opportunity to ride in her car.

"We'll know either tomorrow evening or Wednesday," Sierra answered.

"I don't know why buckethead he_____ out," she said, teasing Jasmine.

Jasmine shut her door and put _____ elt. "Because I'm waiting to try out f_____erlea ers, that's why."

"Come on now. We all know you c___ dance."

Jasmine sounded irritated. "Please. Let's not go into any more dance jokes."

Jasmine could dish out the jabs but she couldn't take them. I listened as Brenda got on her nerves. I should have felt sorry for Jasmine, but I didn't. I'm sure Sierra felt the same way; especially after the things Jasmine had said about Sierra on Friday night.

My house was the closest, so Brenda dropped me off first. "I'll talk to y'all tomorrow. I need to study for this test and try not to worry about our audition."

They waited for me to get inside the house. I waved. Ms. Pearl exited the dining room as I neared the stairs. "How did it go?"

"I won't know until tomorrow or Wednesday."

"Well, I left your food on a plate in the microwave. It should still be warm."

"Where's Mom? Dad?" I asked.

"Your mom wasn't feeling well and your dad had some event he needed to be at."

Just an average day in the Franklin household.

~ 13 ~

Daddy's Girl

Homework kicked my butt. It took me an hour longer than I thought it would to finish my math. I closed the tablet, threw it in my backpack, and flopped on the bed. I hoped my mom didn't hear my phone ring because she didn't like me taking calls after nine and it was nine-thirty. I hoped she was asleep as I answered the phone.

"May I speak to Britney?" a male's voice came across from the other end.

I recognized Marcus's voice immediate. "It depends on whose calling?" I teased.

"It's me. Marcus from school."

I laid on my back and talked to Marcus as we got better acquainted. I was hesitant to tell him who my dad was. Sometimes, folks would try to get to know me only with hopes of getting close to my dad, thinking he could make them a star. I learned that as early as elementary school. I decided to keep that piece of information about my dad to myself; at least for now. We ended up talking until about midnight.

I paid for it the next morning. My mom shook me several times and yanked the covers off me. She picked up my phone that lay by my side. "So this is why you couldn't get up? I'm taking your phone," she said as she pulled me out of the bed.

"But Mama," I responded, my eyes barely open.

"But Mama nothing. You're too old for me to have to monitor when you get up and when you don't. Your alarm has been going off for thirty minutes."

I glanced at my clock with one eye open. "Oh. I still have twenty minutes."

"I'll just have to write you an excuse because I'm not going to kill myself trying to drive you to school on time."

An hour and a half later, I walked into my homeroom class and handed Mrs. Johnson the handwritten excuse from my mom. She glanced at it and gave me permission to take a seat. I held my head down as I walked past my classmates. "Ms. McNeil, can you tell Ms. Franklin what we were discussing before she graced us with her presence?"

I knew there was a reason why I didn't like Mrs.

Johnson. She could be a butthole when she wanted to be. I tuned out Jasmine and thought about my conversation with Marcus. I couldn't wait to see him. "Do you have any questions?" Mrs. Johnson asked, interrupting my daydream.

"No ma'am," I responded.

"The test will be this Friday." She wrote an assignment on the chalk board. "I was disappointed in your quiz grades, so I hope you all do better on the test."

Jasmine mimicked her. I laughed. "And for those of you who think you're funny, I suggest you use that energy studying instead of telling jokes."

Jasmine looked at me as if wondering how she knew. I shrugged my shoulders and mouthed the words, "I don't know."

Homeroom ended, and I met Jasmine and Sierra after class. Before I could tell them about the conversation I'd had with Marcus the night before, Jasmine blasted out she talked to DJ. "About what?" Sierra asked.

"Nothing really. We just talked. You know, stuff that girls and boys talk about."

Sierra remained quiet. I wondered myself if Jasmine actually spoke with him or if she only said it to upset Sierra. "I'll catch y'all later. I need to take a bathroom break before I head to my next class," I said. If they were going to argue, it would be without me refereeing. I had too many other things on my mind than to deal with their drama.

Tanisha blocked the mirror as I exited the bathroom stall. "Excuse me," I said.

She didn't move. Arguing with her this early in the day was also out of the question. She needed the mirror more than I did. As I was walking away, she commented, "Look at those shoes. My little sister has shoes way better looking than those."

I stopped a few steps away from the door. I turned and said, "Even wearing a uniform, my entire ensemble," my index finger went up and down, "cost more than your whole wardrobe."

"Please. You can barely afford the uniform you have on your back."

I turned completely around. "I know I'm new and things but you must not know who my daddy is. He is the one and only Teddy Franklin so trust me, I can afford to buy you and your whole crew a new wardrobe. And trust me, you definitely could use one."

The stunned look on her face was priceless. The girls standing around said things like, "Wow. That's her dad. Ooh. He still looks good. I read about him on the Young, Black, and Famous blog."

I left them going back and forth about the things they thought they knew about my dad. I rushed out the door hoping I wouldn't be late for class. I barely made it through the door before the tardy bell rang. Tanisha made me sick and if I didn't watch it, she would also get me into trouble. Something about her brought out the worst in me.

The rest of the day went by fast. The major highlight of the day was having Marcus walk me to my last class. He was such a gentleman, and my heart fluttered whenever he was around. We weren't girlfriend-and-boyfriend, but I sure hoped we were leading to it. I had to pump myself up so I could ask him to the Sadie Hawkins dance. *But what if he says no? I don't think I could take the rejection.*

~ 14 ~

Ms. Popular

My mom was on my s-list; the list that folks go on when I'm mad at them. *Why did she have to take my phone? This is the wrong time because I need to talk to Marcus.* I was still upset about the baby news my parents dropped in my lap, so my mom should have been trying to stay on my good side. *Whoever heard of someone waiting fourteen years to have another kid?* She and my dad must have lost their minds. What were they thinking? *If they think I'm going to be babysitting the snotty-nosed rugrat, they have another think coming.* I tried to study, but couldn't concentrate. I knocked on my parents' bedroom door. I learned a long time ago not to barge in. Once I did and got a sight of them both in a position that made me want to puke.

"Come in," my mom yelled. Their bedroom looked like a mini-apartment. The king-sized bed was to the right of the room, but one section had a chaise, a desk, and a huge bookshelf along with an entertainment center and a plasma TV almost as big as the one in the living room. My mom was dressed in her silk pajamas and my dad was on the phone, probably wheeling and dealing. I sometimes wondered when did he ever sleep.

I sat on the edge of the bed near my mom. "Can I have my phone back, please?" I begged.

"Destiny, go on and give the girl back her phone," he said as he threw his cell phone on the bed.

"See, that's the problem right there. You're always giving the child everything she wants."

"And what's wrong with that? She knows if she doesn't get up on time in the morning, that butt is mine."

My dad had spanked me only one time. I fell on the floor like he had killed me, and it scared him so much he never whooped me again. Now Mom, well, let's just say she only recently retired laying her hands on me. Her idea of punishment now resulted in her taking some of my things away.

I patiently waited for them to go back and forth. My mom caved in and handed me my cell phone. I couldn't stop the grin from forming on my face. "I love you, Mama," I said, as I hugged and kissed her on the cheek.

She tried to push me away. "Love you too, but you heard your dad. Tomorrow morning you better have your butt up on time."

I went to the other side of the bed and hugged and kissed my dad on the cheek. "Love you too, Daddy. You're the greatest."

"And you know this."

I skipped to my room. As soon as I closed my door, I turned the phone on. I felt so much better. I had several messages. Marcus had called. I didn't want him to think I would be available every time he called me so I decided to wait until I saw him the next day to talk to him. I dialed Sierra's number.

"Girl, I've been trying to reach you all night."

"My mom had my phone, but thanks to my dad I got it back."

"Well, your friend Jasmine has lost her doggone mind."

"Uh. She's your friend too."

"Not the way she's been acting."

"What now?" I asked. I lay across my bed to hear about the new drama.

"She went ahead and asked DJ to the dance."

Wow. Jasmine didn't waste any time. "Did she tell you that?"

"No. DJ was the one who told me. Do you know how that made me look?"

"Yes, that was kind of foul. She could have told you."

"Exactly. Wait until I see her tomorrow."

"Calm down." I pictured her face turning beet red.

"She's just as bad as Tanisha. I mean, how could she stab me in the back?"

I listened to her go on and on about how two-faced she thought Jasmine was. She was correct, but then again, that's what Sierra got for competing for the same guy. I had to do something. DJ had to know this would cause some tension. He knew we were all friends. He saw us walking together every morning and sitting together at lunch. After hanging up with Sierra, I called Jasmine. She didn't answer her phone the first time I called so I called her again.

"Jas, you got some explaining to do."

"I'm innocent," she blurted out.

"What's going on with you? Since we got to Plano High, you've been riding Sierra hard."

"If she's going to be a part of our crew, she needs to step up her 'A' game."

"Girl, Sierra is who she is and there's nothing wrong with her. I don't know what kick you're on, but get off it. Please."

"So she ratted to you about DJ?"

"You should have told her you asked him. Now she feels rejected."

"That's not my fault."

"Well you could have told her."

"Maybe. Maybe not. Now she knows."

Jasmine better have been glad we weren't talking face-to-face. I was all for Sierra slapping some sense into her. Now Jasmine had two of us mad at her. I slammed the phone down without responding.

~ 15 ~

A Girl's Best Friend

Wednesday morning, I woke up on time and beat both of my parents downstairs. I was back in my mom's good graces. She talked my ear off on the way to school. I couldn't repeat what she said because my mind was on the situation with Sierra and Jasmine.

Sierra sat on the stairway near the front of the school building. I took a seat next to her. She looked like she had been crying. We talked about everything except Jasmine. The first homeroom bell rang. We were picking up our stuff when Jasmine walked up to us and handed us each a bag of Godiva chocolate. "Can I get some love?"

"Don't think this chocolate is going to make up for what you did," Sierra said.

"I have your favorite. The ones with the nuts."

"While you two figure it out, I'm going to take a bite out of some of mine before I get to class." I removed a few pieces of candy and put the rest in my backpack. I didn't want the teacher to have any excuse to confiscate it. Mrs. Johnson would do it just so she could eat it herself.

I bumped into Marcus after second period. "Did you make it?" he asked.

I must have had a confused look on my face because he went on to say, "The dance tryouts. The results have been posted."

"What?" I got excited. I couldn't stand still. "No. I need to go find Sierra." I glanced at my watch. "Dang it. I'll be tardy if I do. I'll go after this class. Thanks."

I hugged him; surprising him and myself. I left him standing there as I entered my class. I was too excited to concentrate on the lecture. After class, I rushed to find Sierra and we ran through the crowd of people to get to the gym. It took us a few minutes to get close enough to see the list of names for the Dancing Diamonds.

"I don't see my name," Sierra said, sounding disappointed.

"Mine either," I echoed.

"We're on the B team," Sierra said, not sure if we should be excited or feel rejected. I didn't respond.

"I see you two made it," Tanisha said as she stood on the sidelines. "I should have made it, but I guess they weren't going for talent this year."

She rolled her head and walked away. Tanisha confirmed it for us. Being on the B team meant we were in. We jumped up and down with excitement. "We did it," we both chanted.

At lunch time, we shared the good news with Jasmine. She seemed excited for us. Things seemed to be going fine between her and Sierra, so we had a pleasant lunch. "I'll see you after school," I said, before going to meet Marcus outside the cafeteria door.

I walked with Marcus to my next class. I was so excited to be a Dancing Diamond. I got over my insecurities from earlier and asked, "Would you like to go to the Sadie Hawkins dance with me?"

"Yes. I've been waiting for you to ask me all week."

"You should have said something."

"And risk you telling me you asked some other dude? No way."

Marcus wasn't afraid to show me his vulnerable side. I found it attractive, and that mixed with his twinkling eyes had me under his spell. I had to snap out of it though, because we were standing outside of my classroom. My first date with a boy and I was a Dancing Diamond. Being in high school was a wonderful thing.

Both of my parents were happy to hear my good news about being a Dancing Diamond. I had to figure out a way to tell them about the dance. I did what my dad would do: I decided to tackle the issue head-on. They were sitting in the den watching TV when I decided to approach the subject. I took a seat in the chair across from them. My dad was massaging my mom's feet. I wondered if Marcus would massage my feet. I wanted a man just like my dad.

"What's going on, sugar foot?" my dad asked.

"The school is having a dance and I need a new outfit."

"No problem. We can go this weekend and find you something," my mom said.

"With all those clothes you have, you should already have something in your closet. I swear you and your mama going to put me in the poor house with all the shopping you like to do."

I looked at my mom for assistance in pleading my case. "Teddy, it's our daughter's first high school dance. She has to have a new dress."

He mumbled some words I couldn't figure out. I tapped my foot on the floor. "There's something else," I said. Both set of eyes were on me. "It's a Sadie Hawkins dance and I asked this guy named Marcus to go with me."

"A date. Oh hell no." My dad pushed my mom's leg

down and faced me completely. "You're only four-teen and you're too young to be going out on dates."

"Dad, please. I already asked him. He said yes. How is that going to make me look?"

My mom reached out to him and rubbed his arm. "Dear, let's discuss this. Bri, go on upstairs. We'll let you know what we decide."

I stormed away. If they told me no, I would be the laughing stock of the school. How would I face everybody? How would I be able to face Marcus? I never wanted anything as much as I wanted them to say yes. I said a quick prayer as I waited on the verdict.

~ 16 ~

Don't Hate

Ibarely slept wondering what my parents would say. It was hard to tell. Although I was a daddy's girl, he was strict when it came to boys. Up until now I didn't care that much about boys, so it never really mattered. Marcus was different. I didn't know why, but I sure wanted to find out.

"Bri, if you're still in that bed, your butt is grounded," my mom yelled from the other side of my bedroom door.

I grabbed my watermelon tube of lip gloss and went to the door fully dressed. "I'm ready.'"

"Good. Your dad wants to talk to you before you leave for school today."

I followed her down the stairs. The aroma of breakfast made my mouth water. I picked up a homemade biscuit and took a bite out of it before taking a seat at the dining room table. My dad's face hid behind the daily *Dallas Morning News* paper.

My mom took a seat across me. He put the paper down and looked me in the eyes. "So tell me about this Marcus."

"He's a sophomore. He's nice. He walks me to class sometimes. He's real smart. I think you would like him."

My mom reached across the table and held my hand. "We've decided to let you go this one time, but under one condition."

I did my best to hold in my excitement. I silently thanked God for answering my prayers. "Thank you, Daddy. You're not going to regret it. I'll come home super early just to prove it."

"Since it's a school dance, you can come home at midnight. That'll give the driver enough time to drop off your date."

"Driver?" I was getting my own driver. Oh, so cool. I couldn't wait to tell the girls.

"I will feel better if I have a driver pick up you and your date. I'll have your mom arrange everything."

I forgot about my breakfast. I jumped up out of my chair and wrapped my arms around his neck. "Thank you. Thank you. I'll do whatever you want. Just name it."

"Baby girl, I just want you to get good grades and be on your best behavior if you know what I mean."

"Yes, Daddy. I promise I won't disappoint you." I kissed him on the cheek.

"You two are something else. Come on girl, so I can get you to school," Destiny said, as she pulled away from the table.

"Where's my sugar?" Teddy asked. My mom blew him a kiss.

"No, that's not going to do."

I walked away to get my backpack. I didn't wait to see them get all mushy. No wonder my mom was having a baby. Enough about them. I was too excited. I couldn't wait to tell my girls about Marcus and my private car and driver. It was going to be on.

Several kids were whispering as I walked down the hall headed to my homeroom class. Marcus stopped me right before I got to the door. "Hey, pretty girl."

"Hey yourself," I responded.

"Want to sit with me at lunch time?"

He knew I normally sat with my girls, but with some of the tension as of late, I decided to take him up on his offer. "Sure."

The morning dragged on. Sierra and Jasmine met me outside of the cafeteria door. "I'm eating lunch with Marcus."

"You're what? Oh, no, you're not dumping us for a guy," Jasmine said.

"I'm not. I asked him to the dance so it's some stuff we need to discuss."

"Looks like everybody has a date to the dance, except for me," Sierra pouted.

Jasmine rolled her eyes. "Whoop-de-doo. I'm going with DJ, but I'm not eating lunch with him."

"That's you. Marcus asked and I accepted." Marcus happened to walk up. "I'll see you two later." I followed Marcus into the cafeteria.

Marcus paid for our lunch. I felt eyes on us as we found us a table far from where his crew and my girls normally sat. He placed his tray on the table and assisted me with my chair. I looked up and saw Tanisha roll her eyes. The smile on my face widened. I guess she wanted my man now, too. During the course of lunch, I tuned out the noise around us and gave Marcus my undivided attention.

Marcus and I were laughing about something as we walked to the hallway. My eyes flew open at the sight of Tanisha and Jasmine both flying off at the mouth in each other's faces. They were so close, I was surprised they weren't throwing bows. I left Marcus's side, and pushed my way past the onlookers. I stood between the two. "What's going on here?"

"You need to tell your girl to stay out my face," Tanisha yelled.

More people were leaving the cafeteria, and a crowd formed around us.

Jasmine's hand was flying all over the place. "Bri, move out the way so I can give her what she's been asking for."

All hell broke loose as they started swinging, ignoring the fact I was there in the middle. I forgot about Marcus and the crowd as I tried to stop them from hitting each other and, more importantly, me. The hall monitor moved through the small crowd and escorted the three of us to the office.

I was pissed. It wasn't even my fight and I was dragged in to see the assistant principal. As we waited, Jasmine pulled out her compact mirror to freshen up. Tanisha crossed her arms and turned her back towards Jasmine and me. "I hope he hurry up. I have a test," Tanisha said.

Mr. Reese was a short, bald man. He didn't seem too much taller than me. We followed him to his spacious office. "So, what happened?"

Each one of us gave our account of what led up to us being escorted to the office. "I was only trying to stop things from escalating out of hand," I insisted.

Jasmine added, "She's telling the truth. This is my and Tanisha's fault. Bri, she didn't do anything."

"Is that true, Tanisha?" Mr. Reese asked.

Tanisha shrugged her shoulders, but didn't say anything.

"Ms. Franklin, you're free to go. Next time, get an adult to assist."

I looked at Jasmine and then at Mr. Reese. "Yes sir."

I jetted out of the office so fast I almost forgot to get my excuse. My phone vibrated as I left the office. I pulled it out my book bag and saw it was a text message from Marcus. He was checking to see how things went. That was sweet of him.

All eyes were on me when I entered my next class. I felt embarrassed, although I hadn't been the one in the altercation. I avoided eye contact with everyone and slid behind my desk.

"Ms. Franklin, don't you have something for me?" my teacher asked.

I retrieved the pass from my bag and placed it in her extended hand. *The next time I get in trouble, it better be for something I really did.*

~ 17 ~

Misdemeanor

Jasmine and Sierra were waiting for me by the flagpole after the last bell rang. I barely got within hearing distance when Jasmine blurted, "Do you know I almost went to jail behind that heifer?"

Shocked, I asked, "What happened?"

"Come to find out if you get in a fight in school, the principal has the right to call the police."

"Man, that's messed up," Sierra said, as she shook her head.

"Well, what happened?" I asked.

"I called my dad on the phone right then and there." She paused, then continued. "Fortunately, he was able to talk him into just giving us detention."

"Lucky for you."

"I almost had a misdemeanor charge."

"Wow, our friend the convict," Sierra teased.

I started singing the chorus to one of Akon's songs. "That's not funny."

Tanisha walked by. They both looked each other up and down. I grabbed Jasmine by the arm and pulled her in the opposite direction. "Come on. Isn't that Brenda over there?" I pointed toward the driveway in front of the school. I didn't see Brenda's red convertible, but I didn't want to visit my friend in jail, either. Sierra and I did our best to diffuse what could have been another volatile situation.

We were standing near the curve, waiting on our prospective rides. "Jas, you got a minute?" DJ asked, walking up.

I looked around, but Marcus was nowhere in sight. Jasmine walked away with DJ. "I wonder what that's all about?" Sierra asked.

"I'm sure she'll tell us." Things seemed cool between Jasmine and Sierra; but Sierra looked pissed that Jasmine and DJ were talking. She couldn't keep her eyes off them.

I looked up after hearing someone call my name. It was my mom waving and trying to get my attention. "I'll see you later," I said. I waved at Jasmine as I left the campus.

During the ride home I recanted the day's events.

"Next time, you let that hot-headed Jasmine handle her own battle," Destiny insisted.

"But . . ."

"But, nothing. You tried to stop her but she didn't want to listen. Don't let me ever hear of you fighting over a boy. You hear me?"

"Yes, ma'am." I felt like I was in trouble and hadn't done anything.

"I mean it. Guys get off on things like that. Do you think it makes you cute? No. All they do is laugh behind your back with their friends. The two girls fighting look stupid and the next thing you know the guy ends up dating someone else. Ain't no man worth fighting over."

I recalled a story I'd overheard about her fighting a groupie because of my dad. I guess she forgot about that incident. I didn't say a word. I listened, *really* listened to her talk about men. I hoped I wouldn't run into the type of guys she talked about; but I made mental note just in case. My mom could be cool when she wanted to be. She almost made me forget about the baby.

I was surfing the Internet when my instant message box popped up from Sierra. I clicked on the link she wanted me to see. Someone had anonymously posted a snippet of Jasmine's fight on the Internet.

Some of the gossip blogs added their twists to it, with her dad being the famous ex-NFL player. Jasmine's number appeared on my cell phone.

"I see it," I said before giving her the opportunity to say anything.

"My mom is pissed. I'm grounded until next weekend, so I won't be able to help you go pick out a dress this weekend."

"Oh man. Well. It'll just be me, my mom, and Sierra."

"Well, you didn't have to sound so disappointed."

"Sorry." I really was sorry. Jasmine could get on my nerves sometimes, but when it came to fashion, she was on point.

I typed messages back and forth with Sierra, while I chatted with Jasmine on the phone. She said something that made me pause. "So you care more about DJ than you're letting on?"

"If I didn't, I wouldn't have been standing up to Tanisha like that. She was all upset that he's going with me to the dance."

"Maybe you should cancel. He's not worth all the trouble."

"And be without a date? I don't think so. This is my first date and it might as well be with one of the most popular boys in school."

"I sort of feel sorry for Sierra," I said.

"There are plenty of guys she can ask."

"She's shy, so I doubt if she gets the nerve up to ask anybody else."

"Then it's her loss. She can just stay at home like the other lonely girls." Jasmine laughed. I didn't.

"Sierra's our friend, and since we're going we should be trying to find her someone to go with."

"Look. We're in high school now and we're not going to be able to do everything together like we did in junior high."

The more I talked to Jasmine, the more she pissed me off. My phone beeped. I ended the call to Jasmine to answer. I didn't care who was on the other end. To my relief, it was Marcus. Marcus and I talked until midnight. I set my alarm thirty minutes earlier, so that way if I did hit the snooze button I would still get up on time. I didn't need to get on punishment like Jasmine this soon before the dance. My dad was just looking for an excuse for me not to go.

"I heard about the little ordeal Jasmine got herself in yesterday," my dad said as I hugged him.

"This girl Tanisha is a trip. She has it in for all of us."

"You know how to handle yourself." My dad looked at me.

"Don't worry. I remember everything you taught me."

"Teddy, don't be condoning fighting," Destiny walked beside him and playfully hit him on the arm.

"I know Rocky didn't say that." He and I laughed as he told some stories of how my mom fought a few groupies. My mom didn't find it funny.

"Get your stuff. It's time to go," she said.

I stopped in the hallway mirror and applied another coat of kiwi-melon lip gloss.

~ 18 ~

The Diva in Red

Sierra didn't seem to mind the fact that Jasmine wasn't going to be part of our shopping spree. I was actually surprised she still wanted to go along, since she didn't have a date herself.

"Now girls, the first rule of shopping for a dress: you want to make sure you find something exclusive. Something you don't have to worry about seeing on anyone else. Since this is just a dance, we won't have something custom made, but we'll go to a boutique because all the other girls will be going to the department stores."

I hadn't thought of that. Mom was good for something. We went to several different boutiques before we found the perfect dress. I twirled around so my mom and Sierra could get the full effect. "Yes, that's the one," my mom said, smiling and tugging in the waist area. "It needs to be taken up about an inch here and we'll get it."

The sales clerk made a note of the changes. I removed the ruby red sleeveless dress and handed it to her. My mom pulled out her credit card and paid for it, while Sierra and I continued to browse the dresses. Before dropping Sierra off, my mom treated us to a meal at Le Bistro's, one of my favorite places to go for a chicken salad sandwich.

Jasmine and Sierra barely spoke the next week, but I was on cloud nine and didn't let their issue interrupt my thoughts. It was Friday, and I had so much to do to get ready for the dance. My mom had someone come to the house to do my hair. The beautician pulled my hair back into a French roll and let a few ringlets fall down on each side of my face. I didn't know if I liked it yet; my face appeared rounder for some reason.

"Let me do your makeup, and then you can get dressed," my mom said as I followed her to her bathroom.

My bathroom was big, but my parents' bathroom was huge. I pulled my chair up to the vanity area. I started picking up various makeup vials. "What about this color?"

My mom removed the eye shadow case from my

hand and placed it back among the many other cases. "Dear, you just sit back and let me."

Twenty minutes later, I looked in the mirror and hardly recognized myself. My face was perfect, from the eye shadow to my lip gloss. My dad knocked on the door before walking in.

"Your date is here."

"He's here? I didn't hear the doorbell ring." I jumped out of my seat.

Destiny said, "Calm down. He can stand to wait a few more minutes."

"Baby girl, you look beautiful."

My dad's approval made my night.

My mom pushed him out the door. "Don't make her cry or she'll mess up her makeup."

"Take your time. It'll give me a chance to learn about Marcus and where his people come from."

My mom attempted to calm me down. "He's just kidding. Marcus will be fine. Come on. I have something else for you."

I admired myself in her bedroom mirror. I hoped Dad wasn't giving Marcus too hard of a time. I didn't want him to dump me before we officially became girlfriend-and-boyfriend.

My mom placed something around my neck. I looked at the reflection of it in the mirror. It was a teardrop diamond ruby necklace. "This is perfect," I said as I waited for her to close the clasp. I hugged her.

"It's time. Let's go rescue Marcus."

I placed a sheer white chiffon shawl around my shoulders and followed her down the stairs. My dad and Marcus were laughing at something when I entered the living room.

Marcus said, "Wow. You look great."

"Close your mouth, son," my father said.

"Sorry, Mr. Franklin," he apologized.

Marcus looked good himself. He impressed me with his gray pin-striped suit and red tie to match my dress. He handed me a small corsage. My mom pinned it on me. "Time to take some pictures," my dad said, pulling out his new digital camera my mom had given him for his birthday.

After what seemed like fifteen minutes of picture taking, my parents walked us out to the black Rolls-Royce waiting to take us to our destination. I felt like Cinderella as I stepped into the car.

"I had no idea when you said your dad was sending a car to pick me up it would be a Rolls and man, these houses are the bomb," Marcus said excitedly.

During the course of our previous conversations I'd failed to mention to Marcus where I lived and what my parents did for a living. My mom had her charities and special projects, and my dad was the once-famous singer, now-famous record executive. To me, living like this was just a way of life, but to some people it would seem special.

"Well, it's nothing. I'm surprised he didn't get us a stretch limo," I responded.

"No. This is cool. Folks are going to be tripping when we pull up in this." He continued to talk. "I didn't know your dad was *the* Teddy Franklin."

"He's just plain Dad to me."

"Well, he's a living legend. Not saying that he's old and things. But I have all of his CDs and the artists that he represents."

So far, our date seemed to be about my father. I didn't know if I should be happy or sad. I listened to Marcus recite my dad's resume, one that I was more than familiar with and really didn't care to hear about now; but I wouldn't interrupt Marcus. I pretended to be interested.

The driver opened our door, and when we exited, people passing by were pointing and commenting. Marcus held his arm out and I held on to it as we walked down the walkway toward the auditorium where the dance was being held. We were definitely the center of attention. I looked good in red, and with Marcus by my side we looked like the perfect couple.

A song by Lil Jon blasted through the speakers. I looked around the dimly lit room to see if I could see

Jasmine. I noticed a few faces from class. I waved at a few people as our eyes locked. Marcus asked, "Would you like some punch?"

My throat felt dry so I took a sip as soon as he handed me a cup of the red punch. Chris Brown's new song came on. "Let's dance," Marcus said. He took both of our cups and set them on a nearby table.

Marcus had a few good moves, but he couldn't outdance me. We were dancing like we were on *106 & Park* when I noticed Tanisha dancing with a guy a few inches shorter than her. He seemed like he was having a good time, but Tanisha's frown showed the opposite. Now that I knew I had an audience, I showed off on the dance floor. Marcus had no problems showing me he knew how to hang.

~ 19 ~

Nothing Like the First Time

The deejay played a slow song. Marcus led me to the dance floor. I hoped he couldn't hear my heartbeat. I tried my best to calm down. This would be my first slow dance. I waited for Marcus to lead. He placed his arms around my waist and I placed my hands on his shoulders. Mariah Carey's voice blasted throughout the room as I closed my eyes and leaned my head on Marcus chest. I could hear his heartbeat and smell his signature cologne.

For those minutes, I imagined it was just me and Marcus. No one else mattered. I didn't know what love felt like, but if it felt like this, it was a great feeling. I hoped Marcus felt the same way. We danced off the next few songs. The deejay quickened the pace with the Ying Yang Twins latest song. We decided to take a break.

"Girl, I almost didn't recognize you," Jasmine said as she and DJ walked up to us. We hugged.

Jasmine looked good in her short, emerald green dress. I would have to ask her later where she'd gotten it. The three-inch heels she wore made her seem slimmer. "When did you get here?" I asked.

"About fifteen minutes ago?" DJ had a hard time getting past security. I forgot to leave his name at the gate.

Another one of my favorite songs played. I grabbed Marcus by the hand, and soon we saw DJ and Jasmine dancing beside us. We had our own dance competition going. Marcus and I won hands down. DJ would need another partner if he wanted to beat us. We danced so much my feet hurt.

"Y'all want to hang out after the dance?" DJ asked Marcus.

Marcus looked at me before responding. I looked at my watch. I remembered what my dad said. I liked Marcus and wanted to be able to see him again outside of school. "We better not. I have to be home by twelve."

Marcus said, "Man, we can get together tomorrow."

Tanisha and her date were standing outside. We

passed them. I hoped Jasmine wouldn't say anything. DJ and Marcus greeted Tanisha, but we just kept walking. "Ooh wee, now that's what I'm talking about!" DJ said loudly.

He walked up to where our driver stood near the Rolls-Royce. "Somebody take my picture."

"Man, that's our ride," Marcus said.

DJ stepped back. "Wait until my dad hears this. Did y'all win the lottery or something?" he asked.

"Naw. Britney's dad rented it for us."

"This is ice."

I glanced at Jasmine. She didn't seem too pleased her date was fawning over our ride home. The driver held our door open. I entered first. I waved at Jasmine and DJ. I could see Tanisha looking on from behind them, jealousy written all over her face.

Marcus and I had a pleasant conversation on the way to his house. Our night ended on a good note. We got to his house too quick in my opinion. The driver held the door open. Marcus leaned down and gave me a quick peck on the lips and exited the car. He had caught me off guard. My hand automatically went to my lips. It was just a quick kiss, but my heart fluttered nonetheless.

My phone rang. It was Marcus. "I had a good time tonight," he said.

"Me too."

"Will you be my girl?" he asked.

Should I or shouldn't I. What was I hesitating for? Of course I would be his girl. After a night like we had, there's no way I was going to pass up being his girlfriend. I responded, "Sure."

"You've made me the happiest guy at Plano High."

We talked until the car pulled up in my driveway. We said our good-byes. "I'll wait until you get inside," the driver said.

I fumbled with my key. My dad opened the door before I could get it in the lock. "You're fifteen minutes early. I'm proud of you."

"Thanks, Dad." I hugged him.

"So did you have a good time?" he asked.

"Yes. Thanks again for letting me go."

"Marcus seems like a nice guy. As long as you keep your grades up, if you want to see him again, I might let you."

"Really." This was working out better than I had planned. "Thank you, Daddy," I said again. I hugged him and left him downstairs.

My mom, dressed in a silk robe, was sitting on my bed when I entered my room. "How was it? Tell me everything." She patted the bed for me to take a seat.

I told her about everything except the kiss. "I was nervous about the dance. I didn't let him get too close."

"That's right. Because if you start letting them touch and feel, they'll want to do other things and you don't want them to disrespect you."

"Yes, ma'am."

"It's late. You've had an exciting night and me and your dad are about to retire."

"Mom," I said, as she walked to the door.

She turned around. "Yes."

"Can you keep it down tonight so I can get some sleep?"

She picked up a teddy bear on my dresser and threw it at me. I ducked. "You're getting too grown for your own good. Good night and cover your ears."

I was sleeping good when my phone woke me up. Without opening my eyes, I fumbled for it. "You still up?" Jasmine said from the other end.

"I was asleep."

"I can talk to you tomorrow then."

"No. You woke me up, so talk." I sat up in the bed. According to the clock, it was one-twenty AM.

"I almost did it tonight."

I wasn't in the mood to decipher codes. "Jas, it's late, so just come out and say what you got to say so we can both get some sleep."

"DJ started rubbing on me and my body started feeling funny, but good. I let him suck on my breasts."

"You did what?"

"I stopped him but, Bri, I didn't really want to. Everything was feeling so good."

"If your mama find out she's going to kill you. Do you want to get pregnant?"

"DJ said that girls don't get pregnant the first time they do it."

"Even I know that's the biggest lie in the book. Remember the field trip your mom took us on? Some of those girls got pregnant the first time." I was getting mad. Jasmine pretended to be more sophisticated than the rest of us, but she could be so naive.

"I would have used a condom."

"What do you know about condoms? You're a virgin. Well, at least I thought you were."

"Of course I'm a virgin." She sounded offended.

"I can't believe you almost gave it up to DJ. Dog Jas. You need to check yourself."

"If I knew you were going to react like this, I would have waited."

I sort of felt bad for going off on her, but we all agreed we would get through high school with our virginity intact. We didn't just vow to each other, but to God. A part of me was curious to know how it felt, but to see my mom or dad disappointed, no way. It wasn't worth the headache. *Besides, one person in this family having a baby is more than enough for me.* "Jas. I'm glad you didn't give in. You deserve so much better than DJ."

"Wait until Marcus tries something. You'll see how hard it is to stop."

"First of all, I don't plan on letting Marcus touch me that way. And secondly, what Marcus and I do is our business."

"Well, you don't have to be all snappy and things."

"It's late. I'll talk to you tomorrow. Glad you didn't do it."

"Me too," I heard Jasmine say before our call ended.

~ 20 ~

The Secret

Jasmine sat with her parents during church service and barely said anything to me afterward. I guess she was still tripping on my response to her text message begging me not to tell Sierra what happened with DJ. We're supposed to be friends. There shouldn't have been any secrets between us. I hated being put in the situation, but I had to respect her wishes.

Monday would be my first day of Dancing Diamond practice. My mom wouldn't be able to pick me up, so Sierra's mom agreed to drop me off at home. Drenched with sweat, I ran my last lap around the gym. We had been working out for an hour and had yet to do any movements that could be considered dancing. Ms. Albright finally decided we needed to learn a dance routine.

"First we'll do it without music. When you have the routine down I will add the music." She hit her stick on the hardwood floor. It clicked a couple of times. "Now watch Misty. Misty, do the whole routine, then break it down."

We sat and watched and I envisioned my body moving to the same steps in my head. "A team," Ms. Albright yelled.

I found out the A team were the upperclassmen and the B team were the freshmen and sophomores. If all went well, I planned on being a Dancing Diamond until I graduated. It took an hour before everyone got the routine. She added the music and we rehearsed it a few times. "Great. Wednesday, I'll add another song."

"I like your moves," Misty said to Sierra.

I'm glad something was going good for her. Lately she seemed a little down. I knew Jasmine and DJ were probably behind the sadness in her eyes. "You never told me how the dance went," Sierra said, after we'd changed clothes and walked to search for her mom.

"I haven't told anyone this, but Marcus kissed me."

"Get out of here." Sierra's face lit up. "So how was it?"

I remembered how it felt, and got mushy inside. "It was just a quick peck on the lips."

"Still. Your first kiss."

"Shhh," I said. By now we were outside by her mom's car. I didn't want her to overhear so she could go back and snitch to my mom.

"Ladies, how did it go?"

Sierra answered for both of us. We talked back and forth on the ride to my house. "See you tomorrow," I said as I exited the car.

Both of my parents were out. Ms. Pearl warmed up my dinner and I ate at the kitchen table. I had another test this week, so I went upstairs to study. Marcus called, and we talked until I heard my parents come up the stairs. I pretended to be asleep. My mom pulled the cover over my shoulders and kissed the top of my head. I moved a little.

The next few weeks I spent most of my time rehearsing for the pre-homecoming event. We were to perform at the pep rally a few hours before homecoming. Jasmine seemed a little standoffish at times, but neither I nor Sierra said anything about it to her.

Sierra came into practice one day with a huge grin on her face. "I'm going to homecoming with DJ."

"Say what?"

"He asked me to the homecoming dance and I said yes."

I had to warn her about DJ. "There's something I need to tell you."

"I know you don't like DJ."

"I have good reason not to. He tried to sleep with Jasmine."

"I don't believe you. Jasmine hasn't said anything about it."

"She told me to keep it to myself, but I can't have you going out with him when I know what he's about."

"I get it. You got Marcus and you don't want nobody else to have someone."

"Sierra, that's not it and you know it."

"I can tell."

"DJ filled Jas up. Jas turned him down but if she hadn't, he would have slept with her."

"You don't have to worry about that with me. We're going to the homecoming dance and all we're going to do is dance."

"Be careful, okay? Make sure you don't go anywhere with him by yourself."

"You act like he's some crazy stalker or something."

"I'm just saying." I decided to drop the subject. I made a note to talk to Marcus about his cousin.

Later on that night I got a call from Jasmine. She yelled from the other end, "How could you tell my secret?"

I should have known Sierra would go run her big mouth. "I didn't want something to happen to her."

"Remind me not to tell you anything else."

"If you dated different guys, you wouldn't have to worry about it." If she wanted to act crazy, I was going to talk to her like she was crazy.

"DJ is my business so stay out of it."

"I can't believe you're ruining our friendship over a dude. You and Sierra are a trip."

"Bri. Let's agree that DJ is off-limits. I like DJ. Sierra likes him. I feel he was mine first, so she should have been the one to back down. Since she didn't, all's fair."

"I'm glad I don't have to worry about this type of drama with Marcus."

Jasmine cleared her throat. "You might want to check your man. I saw him talking to some chick after fourth hour the other day."

I didn't give in to the doubt Jasmine was trying to put in my mind. Marcus wasn't like DJ and I wasn't going to entertain her nonsense. "You stay out of my business and I'll stay out of yours."

The conversation was dry afterwards. I finally decided to end the call. *Is Jasmine telling the truth? Is Marcus tired of being my boyfriend already?* I tried to erase the negative thoughts from my mind, but I tossed and turned all night. I had nightmares of

Marcus breaking up with me in the middle of the hallway in front of everybody.

"Young lady, you need to remove those shades unless they are prescribed," Mrs. Johnson said when I entered homeroom.

I removed the shades, hoping the bags under my eyes had disappeared. "Put them back on," one of my classmates joked.

Jasmine dropped a note on my desk before going to her seat. I opened it and read it before the tardy bell rang. She was a trip. She called herself apologizing but she still felt like I shouldn't have told Sierra. *Whatever*. I was tired of her.

I was one of the last ones to leave the class. I wanted to avoid my friends. Marcus stood outside waiting on me. "What's wrong?" he asked, as if he had a radar on my senses.

"Let me ask you something. How many girls does DJ see?"

"Where is this coming from?"

"My two best friends are stressing me out because they both like DJ," I blurted. I wasn't supposed to talk about it with him, but I was tired of the mess going on.

"If I were you, I would tell them to leave him alone. DJ got so many girls I lost count."

"That's what I thought."

"But I do have to say this. He's not the one going after them; they are coming after him."

"So it's not his fault that he's a player."

"I'm not saying that. I'm just saying he's not going around asking all these girls out. The girls are asking him out. They buy him stuff, and I'm talking expensive stuff, too."

I don't know why I got mad at Marcus, but the fact that DJ was no saint made me wonder about him. *Is he pretending to like me? Does he have a secret motive?* I tried to ignore Jasmine's nagging voice in my head. The thought of Marcus talking to another girl hurt me. I hoped it was just a nasty rumor.

~ 21 ~

Go Diamonds!

It was the second month of my freshman year and my life had changed tremendously. Jasmine, Sierra, and I were supposed to be the three amigos. We had the diva creed: "One for all." But lately it seemed as if we were all going in different directions. There was one person I blamed for this and his name is DJ. I tried talking to Marcus about it, but he's his first cousin and he can't understand why I don't like him. To quote Marcus, "It's not like you're the one going out with him, so why do you care?"

Sierra and Jasmine were my friends, and because of DJ, the tension between the three of us had mounted to an all-time high. Things just weren't the same anymore. Jasmine's remarks about Sierra's weight had gotten worse. Sierra didn't make the situation better by constantly talking about what she planned to wear on her date with DJ.

I dressed for the pep rally. I hoped I didn't trip. Marcus, my parents, and hundreds of others would be in the stands watching us. While we waited for our turn to enter the gym, Sierra asked, "Did you hear Jasmine is the freshman Homecoming Queen because Tina has a stomach virus?"

Jasmine had been the runner-up. I hadn't heard the news. That was good to hear. I was sure Jasmine wouldn't have a problem stepping in to fill Tina's shoes. I felt bad about it, though, because I would be hurt if I got sick before my big day.

Ms. Albright introduced us to the hyped crowd. Misty was our dance team leader so we followed her lead. By the time our routine was over, I was too hyped to sit down. I ran up to where my parents sat and gave them a hug. "Baby girl, you did good," my dad said with pride.

My mom ran her hand through my hair. "You remind me so much of me at your age."

Marcus walked over to my parents. Teddy asked, "Marcus, you're invited to dinner tonight. Then you guys can leave for the dance."

I looked at Marcus, hoping he would say yes. He responded, "Sure. I just need to check with my folks first."

My dad was pleased with his answer. "I'll send a car to pick you up."

I said my good-byes to my parents and Marcus, and followed the rest of the Dancing Diamonds to the dressing room to change my clothes. Sierra was standing by our lockers. Instead of getting dressed, she sat bent over with her head in her hands.

I placed my arm around her back. She looked up, and I saw her red, tear-stained eyes. "What's wrong?"

"I saw DJ kissing some other girl."

The jerk. I knew he would do something to hurt her. I don't care if he is Marcus's cousin. The next time I see him I'm going to tell him a thing or two. I reached out to comfort her. "What did he say when you confronted him?"

"He doesn't know I saw him."

"You're not going to the dance with him are you?"

She looked away. "I don't know. Maybe. I haven't thought about it much."

Sure she hadn't. She'd thought about it, or she wouldn't be in here tripping off him. "You can come with me and Marcus."

The tears from her eyes stopped. "Oh, I don't think so."

"Forget DJ."

"I'll think about it."

We dressed, and went our separate ways afterward. My parents were waiting for me outside so I rode home with them. It took me a few hours to get ready for the homecoming dance. I dressed in a smoky gray, form-fitting dress that flared out at the bottom.

Marcus wore a gray suit. We looked cute together. He made me so proud the way he carried himself over dinner. My parents seemed to like him, too, and that was a relief. My dad insisted on taking pictures; afterward we were on our way to the homecoming dance. I checked my cell phone several times, but never got a message from Sierra.

The dance was at full blast when we got there. Some of my favorite songs played, but I didn't want to sweat too much so I turned Marcus down on a few of them. We stood in the long line to take pictures.

Jasmine walked over to us with her date, the same guy who had escorted her out on stage earlier. "Britney and Marcus, I want you to meet Ian. His dad is the quarterback for the Cowboys."

Marcus reached out to shake his hand. "Yo, man. That was a good game Sunday."

Jasmine stood next to me. "So what do you think? He's a hottie and should make DJ jealous."

Here she stood with a guy almost as cute as my man and she was worried about DJ. Things were about to get awkward. DJ and Sierra were headed in our direction.

~ 22 ~

Homecoming

Jasmine plastered on a smile. "Sierra, you look. . . .
You look full."

"Your tiara's a little crooked," she responded.

Jasmine's hand flew straight to the tiara to adjust
it. DJ talked to Ian and Marcus as the line for pictures slowly moved. "What time do you have to be
home tonight?" Sierra asked me.

"Midnight. Nothing's changed."

"Well, we're going downtown when we leave here
so if you guys want to tag along."

Jasmine answered first. "I can't. Ian's leaving to go
out of town tomorrow so he has to be home early."

"I guess it'll just be me and DJ."

Jasmine said, "Don't do anything I wouldn't do."
She grabbed Ian's hand and led him away.

Sierra looked upset. The frowns left when DJ asked her to dance. By now, Marcus and I were next in line to get our picture taken. We posed, looking like a prince and princess. We took several shots. Marcus paid for the pictures and we waited for them to be printed out. He also bought a disk. I placed the disk in my purse. Now that our pictures had been taken, I could dance until I got tired. I grabbed Marcus's arm. "I have to go to the bathroom. I'll meet you over there."

The line wasn't long in the bathroom, so after I freshened up and relieved my bladder, I went to search for Marcus. He wasn't in the auditorium, so I checked outside just in case he'd decided to get some fresh air. I was nearing a corner when I overheard some male voices; one of which was Marcus's. His friends were teasing him about us.

"Man, I heard her dad got major loot," I heard one guy say.

"I'm not dating her because of her dad," Marcus responded.

My body released the tension. Another guy said, "Are you going to give her dad the demo tape?"

"In due time. I can't just drop it on him like that."

"Well, hurry up man. I got this other dude who might be interested, but if you can get Teddy Franklin, forget the other dude."

"I can't just come out and ask him."

"Well, do what you have to do. The clock is tick-ing."

Was Marcus using me to get a demo tape to my dad? It sure sounded like it to me. Well, he could just hang it up. I was out of here. I bumped into DJ. "Slow down, girl."

"Move out of my way."

I stormed around him. I heard him say something to Marcus. Marcus yelled out my name a few times. I ignored him. Here I thought he liked me for me, but he was trying to use me the whole time. I walked out-side and found the driver. Marcus ran behind me.

"Wait. I didn't know you were ready to go."

"You wouldn't because you were so busy talking to your boys about your demo tape."

"Oh that. That's nothing."

"If it's up to me, my dad will never *ever* hear your demo tape."

"What are you talking about, Bri?"

"I know what you're doing. You only wanted to get close to me because you thought my dad would give you a break."

The door to the Rolls-Royce stood open. I entered and Marcus jumped in behind me. "We need to talk. I don't know what you thought you overheard, but it's not even like that."

"Don't say another word to me."

"Calm down, please," he begged, batting his puppy dog eyes.

I could feel myself melting. No, I would not give in. I heard him with my own two ears. I listened to him beg and plead, but as far as I was concerned he was spitting out hot air. He reached for my hand. I jerked it away.

"Bri, did you hear anything I said?"

"Truthfully, no. I stopped listening when I heard you talking to your boys back there."

"I'm telling you the truth. I don't have to lie."

"You made me feel like a fool. And that's unforgivable."

"I'm sorry. The guys were teasing me about how I follow you around like a puppy dog."

"Whatever, Marcus."

"Don't break up with me. I think I love you," he confessed.

My mouth closed because I didn't know what to say after hearing those words. "Love."

"Yes, Bri. I think I love you and if you break up with me I don't know what I'll do."

I laughed. He sure was trying hard to get the demo to my dad. His trick was not going to work. Too much had been said. I didn't know what the truth was. Marcus was dropped off at home. I needed to talk to someone; someone other than him. I knew Jasmine and Sierra were still out, but I left them both messages anyway. It didn't matter what time they called me back, because one thing was for sure: I knew I wouldn't be getting any sleep any time soon. This was supposed to have been a special night, and Marcus ruined it. We had only been a couple for a month and already there was trouble in paradise.

~ 23 ~

P.S. I Love You

I lied to my parents about having a good night. I listened to music as I waited for one of my friends to call. If they didn't call me, I would have to think about getting me a new set of friends. Marcus had left me several messages, but he was the last person I wanted to talk to.

My phone rang just when I dozed off. "I got your message. What's going on?" Jasmine asked.

I repeated to her the things I'd heard. "Do you think I should believe him?"

"I'm not sure. I need to hear his side of the story."

"I'm telling you what I heard. Oh, and get this: He had the nerve to tell me tonight he thinks he loves me."

Jasmine didn't say anything. I called her name a

few times. "He loves you. Don't fall for it. Brenda says guys do that to get our guards down."

"She might be right."

"So are you going to break up with him?"

"I'm not sure. If he's just with me because of my dad, then yes. But what if he really does like me?"

"I'll call DJ and find out tomorrow."

"Speaking of DJ, I wonder if Sierra made it back home yet."

"I don't know. I called her and left her a message before I called you."

"Jas, thanks for listening. I'll let you go. We have a full day tomorrow."

"I can't wait for the game."

"I might not go."

"Girl, you have to. We get to show them girls how to dress."

"I'll let you know."

I stayed in bed Saturday as long as I could. My mom knocked on my door and entered before I could tell her to come in. "You going to sleep all day or what?"

I wiped my eyes as I sat up in bed. "No, ma'am."

She sat on the edge of my bed. "So tell me more about the dance. You seemed to be in a rush to get to your room last night."

My eyes watered. "Mom, there's nothing more to tell."

"Oh no. I know that look. What did Marcus do?" she asked.

This was not the type of conversation I wanted to be having with my mama. What if me and Marcus made up? She would tell my dad and then I would be banned from seeing him. I couldn't take that chance. I decided to tell her something, but it wouldn't be about Marcus.

"Things aren't the same with Jas and Sierra. All because of this guy." I talked to her briefly about DJ. I would rather her be in their business than in mine.

"I thought you girls were smarter than that. Looks like they've broken the cardinal rule of never ever letting a guy come between your friendship."

"Jas also likes to make snide remarks about Sierra's weight."

"Sierra is not as slim as you and Jasmine, but she's at a healthy size. There's nothing wrong with how she looks. She'll just have to watch her weight closer than you two."

"That's what I'm saying. But Jas makes it seem like she's three hundred pounds or something."

"Even if she were, that's not Jasmine's right to talk about her. I might need to have a talk with her mother. Jasmine needs to realize everybody isn't meant to look the same."

She held her stomach. "This morning sickness is kicking my butt."

Before I could make a comment, she rushed off. I followed her to the bathroom next to my room. I turned my head away after seeing her doubled over the toilet. She ran the water in the sink and freshened up. "See, you don't have to worry about this for a long time." She looked at me as she passed by. "At least I hope so anyway."

If this was what you had to go through to have a baby, she didn't have to worry about me doing anything to get in her position. I showered, and stayed in my room most of the day. I still hadn't decided on whether or not I was going to homecoming. Time was ticking, so I needed to make up my mind fast.

I dialed Sierra's number. She answered on the third ring. "I was going to call you, but I'm on punishment."

"You must have missed curfew."

"DJ got drunk and I wouldn't let him drive me home. Brenda had to come get me."

"You called Jas and didn't call me?" Now my feelings were hurt.

"It's not like you have a car."

"I know. But still. I'm surprised Jas didn't call to tell me."

"Me too. I could tell she was thrilled about the way things went down."

"She has to understand. Your mama got killed by a drunk driver so I don't blame you for not letting him bring you home."

"My dad was waiting on me when I got here. I had to listen to him lecture for about an hour. I can't go to the homecoming game. I can't do anything for a whole month."

"That's messed up. I was just thinking about whether or not I was going. I can come over and keep you company."

"I can't have company for a month either, and our sleepover this month is cancelled."

Man. Sierra got it bad. That's why I made sure I made it back before curfew. I didn't want that type of drama. Her dad was strict enough, and now this. I was sure I would be hearing about this from my mom later.

My text message indicator sounded. I read it while continuing my conversation with Sierra. It was Marcus apologizing again for last night. He sent an animated heart and wrote "P.S. I love you."

~ 24 ~

The Weekend

I decided to go to the homecoming game. Jasmine and I were the two best dressed there. I didn't include Brenda in my observation. I purposely ignored Marcus. He pretended it didn't phase him, but I know it did. He still bought me something to drink and snack on. He sent DJ to deliver the items. I took them and didn't send a message back.

"Now, you can't accept his food and not say anything to him," Brenda said.

"I'll think about talking to him." I paused. "I thought about it. Not."

The crowd went wild when our team scored the winning touchdown. We gathered our stuff and headed down the stairs. "Bri, wait up," Marcus yelled.

I kept on walking. "Are you going to avoid me all weekend?"

"If that's what it takes."

DJ said, "Man, don't be running behind her."

I stopped at the bottom of the steps and turned around to face DJ. I didn't care who saw me. "This is between Marcus and me, you drunk bastard."

"You better get your girl before I lay some hands on her." He moved closer to me, but Marcus jumped in between us.

I tried to move Marcus out the way. "No, don't stop him. Let him try to hit me and I'll lay him out."

"DJ, man, chill."

"You picking a girl over your own blood. That's messed up."

Marcus tried to calm us both down. Brenda grabbed my arm. "Come on. Let's go."

I couldn't believe I let DJ get me to the point of acting like a fool in public. That was one thing a diva never did. Although I was mad at Marcus, I was glad he did have the balls to stand up to his cousin. I decided I would take his call If he called me later.

Jasmine went on and on about the scene at the stadium. "Girl, I thought you were going to go upside DJ's head. Good thing Marcus stepped in between y'all."

"DJ's a punk and I don't see what you or Sierra see in him."

Brenda added, "I thought you had better taste than that, Jas."

"But . . ." Jas stuttered.

"But nothing. I went through the spell where I wanted a bad boy. Well, you know what? Only thing a bad boy did for me was get me in trouble."

"DJ's really not like that. He was just standing up for himself."

"Any man who will step to a girl ain't worth a grain of salt."

"Bri did smart off at him," Jasmine said in his defense.

I was too frustrated and tired to get mad at her.

"Silly girl. You try to act like you so grown and you still have a lot to learn." Brenda laughed. She turned up the volume on her stereo and let the top down on the Mustang. I let the wind blow through my hair, and hoped my troubles would blow away like the night breeze.

Marcus called me less than an hour after I made it home. He pled his case again. "Give me another chance, please."

"I'll think about it."

"When will you let me know?"

"At school Monday."

"I love you, Bri. I mean it. I've never said that to any other girl."

"I believe you."

"Then believe what you heard was all a misunderstanding. I don't even sing or rap. That's DJ's thing."

"Let's not talk about your trifling cousin DJ."

"Sorry about that, too. He can be a jerk."

"Jerk isn't the word I would use to describe him."

"He said he's going to apologize to you when he sees you."

"He can keep his apology. Did he tell you he got drunk last night and left my girl stranded?" Marcus got quiet. "That's what I thought. He's trifling."

"My father's throwing a barbecue. He said I can invite anybody I want. I wanted to see if you and your parents could come."

"I'll ask, but can't make any promises."

"Okay. Well, let me know so I can let him know."

We talked for a few more minutes and then got off the phone. I was confused. So much stuff had happened in a short period of time. I didn't know what to believe when it came to Marcus. *He sounded sincere, but is it just a front? Is he more like his cousin DJ than I realized?* I liked Marcus but I was not going to let him use me. For now I would still deal with him, but my guard would be up.

~ 25 ~

The Monday After

Ididn't speak to Sierra the rest of the weekend, so when I saw her on Monday morning standing near the flagpole, we had a lot of catching up to do. "DJ sent me a message and apologized for everything."

"Whoop-de-do. I wouldn't talk to him if I were you."

"Well, I forgive him."

I looked at Sierra. *Where had my friend gone?* This had to be a creature from another planet standing before me. "Sierra, I can't believe you. Between you and Jas, you're going to drive me crazy."

"You got Marcus so you need to chill."

"He pursued me. I didn't go after him."

"If it wasn't for your daddy being a celebrity, he wouldn't have," she snapped.

My mouth dropped open. This was the first time I wanted to slap my best friend. Jasmine, yes, she always said something that made you want to slap her; but Sierra? I couldn't believe she opened up her mouth to say what she said. *Has DJ been telling her some things? Maybe Marcus is lying.*

My mind was all over the place during first period. I probably missed several questions on the pop quiz because I couldn't stop thinking about the situation with Marcus. I lagged behind my classmates as they left the room. Jasmine and Sierra stayed behind too.

"So what's up with you and Marcus? You going to break up with him?" Jasmine blurted out.

I didn't get a chance to respond to her question because Marcus was waiting for me outside the door. "I'll catch up with y'all later," I said.

Marcus avoided eye contact. "Hey beautiful."

"Hey yourself."

We both stood there looking goofy. The second bell rang to indicate we only had a few minutes to get to our next class before being tardy.

"Do you forgive me?" he asked as he walked toward our next class.

"Maybe." It all depended on whether or not I thought he was telling me the truth.

He handed me a bulky envelope. "Read this and it'll explain what I couldn't."

He left me standing outside my class. I rushed to my desk so I could open it before class started. A tube of lip gloss fell out of the envelope when I opened it. Hmm. I checked to make sure the seal hadn't been broken, and placed the cherry-flavored lip gloss to the side. I read Marcus's letter. He apologized again and confessed how he felt about me.

My heart fluttered and all was forgiven. I couldn't wait to see him after class. I was disappointed when I didn't. In between my other classes I wrote him a note. I wouldn't dare tell him I loved him because being in a relationship was all new to me, but I did feel something and it made me feel good.

At lunch time I decided to sit with my girls so we could have a heart-to-heart. I slipped Marcus my note when I passed his table. "Let's eat together," he insisted.

"I'll see you afterwards," I responded.

I could tell he was disappointed, but I'm sure he would feel better after he read my note. I twisted to the table where Jasmine and Sierra sat. "So what's up?" I asked as I placed my tray on the table.

"It's all about you," Jasmine responded.

I snapped my fingers. "Don't hate."

"Seriously, it's all about you." Jasmine went on to tell me about the rumors.

"Wow. So now the word's out about who my dad is and everybody's talking. Oh, well. It's no big deal."

"Don't be surprised if more and more folks try to be your friend now," Sierra said between bites.

"You of all people should know I'm not that gullible," I responded.

"I'm just saying," she said without looking up.

"Well, we all have famous dads, so what. Nobody's tripping that my dad was the star quarterback for the Cowboys until he retired," Jasmine added.

I didn't like people trying to get in my space due to my dad's fame. Sometimes the adults acted crazier than the kids. Being a child of a public person brought on its own share of problems. That's why I struggled with wondering if Marcus's interest in me was sincere. I went with my gut and, as I'd written in my letter, I was giving him a chance; a chance to show me that he cared about me for me, and not for who my dad was.

~ 26 ~

The Family

Why did my parents agree to go to this barbecue over at Marcus's parents' house? It was September in Texas, and hot. Wearing pants or jeans was out. I needed something cool to wear because I didn't know how long we would be outside fighting the heat and flies. I went through several outfits before finding the perfect pink shorts set. I checked my reflection in the mirror. It had to pass my dad's test of not rising too high up the butt cheeks, but I wanted it to be sexy enough to make Marcus and whatever other boys would be around sweat.

Brenda dropped Jasmine off just in time. She had on a cute white short skirt set. My mom would cringe, because according to her a real southern woman wouldn't wear white after labor day. To us, that rule was old fashioned, so we ignored it.

Too bad Sierra was still on punishment. I'm glad Jasmine agreed to go, because I needed her there for support. This would be my first time meeting Marcus's parents, and I didn't know what kind of drama I would face if my parents didn't get along with them. Jasmine and I chatted in the back seat of the SUV as my parents chatted up front. I used Jasmine's mirror to re-apply some lip gloss just as we pulled up in the driveway. Marcus's parents weren't rich, but they weren't poor, either. The driveway was filled with foreign and American cars. We could smell the aroma from the grill when we exited the SUV.

My dad rang the doorbell. People were talking and music was playing. A short woman wearing an apron opened the door. "You must be the Franklins. Come on in."

They all shook hands. "You're the young lady my boy can't stop talking about. Welcome."

Instead of a handshake, she gave me a tight hug. She led us through their house. I could tell my mom was checking things out by the motion of her head as Mrs. Johnson opened the patio door leading to the backyard. She introduced us to this handsome man standing behind the grill. I could see where Marcus got his good looks. I think Jasmine and I were both drooling because Mr. Johnson had it going on. Good looks obviously ran in the Johnson family.

I felt a pair of hands over my eyes. I knew it was Marcus from the smell of his cologne. He led Jasmine and me over to where some more teenagers were hanging out and introduced us. DJ barely opened his mouth to speak, but he gave Jasmine a big old smile. She ate it up, too, because she left me standing to go sit by him.

"I thought you weren't coming at first," Marcus said as we stood there.

"When my dad tells me he's going to do something, he usually does," I responded.

"Want something to drink?" he asked.

"A Sprite would be fine."

"Jasmine, you want something to drink?" he asked.

"I'm cool," she responded.

I took a seat next to one of his cousins while he went to get us something to drink. "Your dad's Teddy Franklin right?" he asked.

The smile on my face turned to a frown. "Yes, and?"

"Marcus has our demo tape but won't give it to him. I thought maybe you could since he's your dad and all."

This guy didn't waste no time. "He's standing over

there next to Mr. Johnson, so why don't you go give him a copy yourself."

"Naw. I ain't trying to get cussed out by my uncle for hounding him."

"That's what I thought," I said as I rolled my eyes and got up from the table.

I met Marcus before he could bring me my drink. "What's wrong? You look like you want to bite someone's head off."

"One of your cousins had the nerve to ask me about giving a demo tape to my dad."

Marcus face turned red. "He did what? Hold these."

He handed me two drinks and marched back over to the table where his cousins were. Everybody pointed to the cousin who had caused all the drama. He and Marcus walked over to where I stood.

"Carlos has something he wants to say to you," Marcus said.

"Bri. I mean, Britney. I apologize for making you feel uncomfortable." He shrugged his shoulder and wouldn't look me in the eyes.

"It's not that I felt uncomfortable, but you don't know me like that to be approaching me about a demo."

"I know. I was out of line. Anything I can do to make it up to you?" he asked.

"We cool."

He extended his hand. I paused a few seconds and shook it.

My mom walked up right then. "What's going on, kids?" she asked.

"Nothing, Mom," I responded.

"Marcus, can you show me where the bathroom is?" she asked.

I followed Carlos back to the area where the other teenagers were hanging out. A few were playing handheld video games when we got back. I walked around the table and sat on the same end as Jasmine and DJ. They were sitting so close I was surprised an adult hadn't come over to say something, but the adults seemed to be in their own little world with the music and laughing going on.

A cute little girl with a head full of ponytails and bows walked over, and handed me her doll. "She's wet," she said in a small squeaky voice.

"She is? Well, let's change her diaper." I played with the little girl.

"Get you some practice, because you're going to be changing plenty of those," Jasmine said.

One of the girls around the table asked, "You pregnant?"

Carlos asked, "Who's pregnant?"

"Nobody." I cut my eyes at Jasmine.

Jasmine ignored me. "Her mom is having a baby."

"Really. Man that's cool," the girl said.

"That's messed up," Carlos said.

DJ popped him on the arm. He continued to say, "I'm just saying. You're, what, a freshman, so you're about fourteen. That's a lot of years between you and your little sister or brother."

I sat there as they talked about how bad their little brothers and sisters were and how they were glad to not be me. They all hoped their parents were through having babies. Marcus came back to the table and sat next to me. He placed his arm around my shoulder. That's when I noticed my dad looking over in our direction, so I kindly slid his arm away. My dad held his beer up to acknowledge the gesture.

~ 27 ~

Backlash

The way Jasmine acted, I would have sworn she was auditioning to be a part of the Johnson family. While we were eating, she made it a point to fawn over DJ. She fed him his food as if he were a helpless baby. She really was making a fool out of herself. I tried to get her to come with me so I could talk to her in private, but she ignored my gestures.

I swatted flies away from my plate and ate my food. Mr. Johnson could throw down on the grill. He could give my dad some competition, but of course I would never reveal that to my dad. My mom taught me one thing: men have shallow egos.

Marcus was attentive to me and made me feel special. I hoped my parents were having a good time because if not, they wouldn't let me see Marcus again. I went to use the restroom, and found Marcus waiting for me outside the door. "Let me show you my bedroom," he said.

"And have my mom or dad kill me; I don't think so."

He held my hand. "Come on. It'll only take a minute."

I looked over my shoulder several times to make sure nobody saw us as he led me to his room. Posters of Ciara and Mariah Carey were plastered on his wall. He retrieved a black box from the desk near his computer and handed it to me. "I was going to wait, but I want you to have it now."

I opened the box and my eyes widened. A gold charm shaped like a dancer stared back at me. I gave him a hug for being so thoughtful. As we pulled away from each other, our eyes locked and we kissed for the second time since we had been dating. There was something different about this kiss. This time, he slid his tongue in my mouth and I floated off the floor.

A knock on the door interrupted us. Fortunately, it was only DJ. "Your dad's looking for you," he said, looking at Marcus.

I wiped the lip gloss from Marcus's lips. "I can't believe we did that and my folks are right outside."

"Calm down, Bri," Marcus said as we strolled out of his room.

My hands were sweaty. "I'm trying. Boy that was close."

He whispered in my ear, "It was worth the risk."

I couldn't help but smile. My mom looked at me suspiciously, (or so I thought) when we exited the house together. I went to sit by her and she just looked at me without saying a word. Her eyes said *we'll talk later*.

Less than an hour later, we were packed up in the SUV headed home. "So did you girls have a good time?" my dad asked.

"Yes, sir," I responded.

My dad stopped at the gas station. As soon as he was out of hearing range, my mom turned around in her seat. "Jasmine, I saw how you were all over that guy DJ."

Jasmine kept looking out the window. My mom continued, "I don't know if I'm going to tell your mother or not; but young lady, you need to have more respect for yourself."

"Ms. Destiny, no disrespect, but I don't think I did anything wrong," she said, turning to face my mom.

"Looks like we need to have a talk about proper etiquette when around boys. Fawning all over a guy like that in public is not proper."

"But—" Jasmine attempted to interrupt.

"But nothing. If you want respect from these

young men, you need to show that you respect your-self."

My dad opened up the door. He fumbled with his wallet. My mom turned back around in her seat. Jasmine looked at me. I didn't know what to say. I turned my head and looked out the window. Jasmine and I sent each other text messages all the way to her house.

"Why your mom tripping?"

"She did have a point."

"What????"

"DJ is a jerk. Why can't you see it?"

"If I didn't know better, I would think you dislike him because you want him for yourself."

I typed "YGTBK," which in text terms meant "you got to be kidding."

"I hope your mom don't tell my mom," she typed.

"She probably won't."

"Will you talk to her for me?"

"I'll think about it."

"Bri, please. Do this and I'll owe you."

I couldn't pass up the opportunity to have Jasmine in my debt. I waited until we got to her house before agreeing to do what she asked. "I'll do it," I said as I hugged her good-bye.

~ 28 ~

Kiss and Tell

The rest of the weekend flew by. I had the Monday morning blues as usual. Sierra paced in front of my third-hour class. "What's up, girl?" I asked.

She grabbed my arm and pulled me to the side as some of the other kids walked by. "DJ told me about the kiss."

My mind didn't register what she was implying. "What do you mean?"

"He told me he walked in on you and Marcus making out."

I wanted to punch DJ out for lying. "We weren't making out. We only kissed. Who else has he been telling this to?"

"I don't know. But I just thought you should know just in case someone else says something about it."

"Thanks, girl, for looking out. Look, I got to go because I can't be tardy again, but I'll see you at lunch."

DJ was telling all my business to Sierra but I'm sure he left, how he and Jasmine were all over each other. When I saw DJ, he was going to get a piece of my mind. I tried to concentrate as the teacher lectured.

Jasmine and Sierra were standing outside the cafeteria door when I turned the corner. "Girl, Sierra told me what happened. Why didn't you tell me about this kiss?" Jasmine asked.

"I didn't have time to."

She pulled out her phone. "You could have called me."

"It was no big deal. It's not like it was the first kiss."

"According to DJ, you two were making out," Jasmine said.

"Well, news flash. Marcus and I did not, I repeat, did not make out." I had lost my appetite. "You two go ahead. I'm going to hang out outside. I'm not hungry."

I left them in front of the door. I walked around the corner and ran right into DJ. "You're just the person I want to see," I said as I stood in front of him with my arms folded.

He stood there with a grin on his face showing all of his teeth. "What's up, Britney?"

"Don't 'what's up' me. You don't know what you walked in on so you need to keep your big mouth shut."

"Marcus told me everything." He walked around me. "I wish I would have hollered at you instead of your friends."

"You're disgusting, and I can't believe Marcus told you anything."

"There's a lot you don't know about my cousin. I bet you he told you he loved you, too, didn't he?" The expression on my face said it all. He continued, "That's what I thought." His stomach growled. "I better go before lunch is over."

I stood there watching DJ as he walked away. "Hey, cutie," Marcus said.

I turned to face him. I slapped him. His hand automatically went to his face. "What was that for?"

"That's for lying." I stormed away.

He walked in front of me. "You owe me an explanation. You just don't lay your hands on someone and walk away."

"Well, I just did. Leave me alone," I said as I walked past him.

"Bri, what now? There's always something going on with you, girl."

"You know what. I'm not even going to entertain you with a response." This time when I walked away, he didn't try to stop me. A part of me was disappointed that he didn't.

After school I had dance practice, so I didn't run into him. Sierra tried to talk to me during our breaks, but I wasn't in the mood to talk to her, either. Besides, I was tempted to tell her about Jasmine and DJ. In fact, since DJ wanted to cause problems in my relationship, I decided it was time to burst his little bubble. While we were changing clothes after rehearsal, I said, "Did DJ tell you he was at the barbecue on Saturday?"

"What about it?"

"If I didn't know better, I would have thought Jas and DJ were a couple."

Sierra's smug expression changed into a frown. "You just can't stand for somebody else to be happy."

"I'm tired of my two best friends being made fools by the likes of DJ."

"You think you know so much, don't you? Well, DJ doesn't want to hurt Jasmine's feelings. That's the only reason he talks to her."

"Oh, really now. That's the same thing Jasmine said he told her about you."

"You're lying," she said, as she threw her stuff in her backpack and stormed away.

I hated to hurt her, but I was tired of walking on eggshells when it concerned DJ. DJ was trying to ruin my life, but have the best of both worlds by playing my friends. *DJ, you've messed with the wrong person.*

~ 29 ~

A Girl Scorned

Marcus was mad at me for slapping him, and I was mad at him for what DJ said, so we went a few days without talking to each other. By Thursday, I hadn't gotten much rest, and was tired of not knowing the state of my relationship with him. I had a big test on Friday and the stress was getting to me.

Jasmine and Sierra were at odds with one another and I was tired of playing mediator. DJ seemed to be the source of all of our problems. Normally, Marcus would have walked me from gym to my last class. My heart ached when I saw him standing outside the gym talking to another girl.

I flew past them. "Bri, wait up," he said.

I refused to stop walking, afraid of what he would say if I did. I rushed into my classroom. Marcus stood outside the door but I wouldn't move out of my seat. The tardy bell rang. He hung his head down low and walked away. The teacher closed the door.

I didn't remember a thing the teacher talked about. All I could think about was Marcus and some other girl. How could he? We weren't officially over, or so I thought. I removed from my bracelet the charm he had given me. After class, I made it a point to walk where I knew he would be waiting. His smile left his face when he looked at the object in my hand. "Bri, we need to talk," he said.

"My mom's waiting on me," I said, without giving him a chance to say anything else.

Tears flowed down my face. I did my best to wipe them before finding my mom parked outside near the curb. "Bri, what's wrong?" my mom asked as soon as I was in the car.

"Nothing," I replied.

She maneuvered through the traffic. "Are you girls fighting again?"

"No, Mom. I told you it's nothing."

"I'm here if you need to talk."

For some reason she thought talking to me about the baby would take my mind off my problems. She didn't realize it only compounded them. I don't mean to sound cold, but the baby was the last thing I wanted to talk about. I would have to deal with it soon enough. I wanted to enjoy it just being me for as long as I could, so why didn't she insist I tell her the problem? She was too quick to change the subject to the baby. The baby this. The baby that. I tried to understand the fascination with the baby, but she was making it difficult.

"Did you hear me? What color do you think I should paint the nursery?"

I rolled my eyes. "Green. Lime green."

"That's a neutral-enough color, but kind of blah. I might just go with yellow."

If she knew what color she wanted, why was she asking me for my opinion? I swear parents can do some stupid things at times. I put my iPod earpiece in my right ear so she couldn't see it, and listened to some songs for the rest of the trip home.

I rushed upstairs, closed my door, and fell across my bed. Life at Plano High wasn't all that good for me these days. My phone beeped. It was Marcus. I answered. "Please stop calling my number," I yelled.

"Bri, I love you and I'm tired of fighting. When you grow up, call me. And by the way, check your e-mail." Marcus hung the phone up without waiting for me to respond.

I looked at the phone. *No he didn't just hang up on me.* I was tempted to call him back and tell him off. I logged on to my computer to see this e-mail he was referring to. I deleted all the spam mail that filled my box. My instant message indicator alerted me that Sierra had logged on to her computer. I ignored it. I scrolled through my e-mail until I came across a message from mjtheballer. I clicked it and read the contents.

Britney, I found out why you slapped me. DJ thought it was funny, but I didn't. I knew you were upset so I wanted to give you a few days to calm down. What you saw after gym today wasn't what you think. I know; it seems like I'm always explaining something. I made the mistake of confiding in DJ my feelings for you. I never told him we were making out. He saw for himself that we only kissed. He thought it was a cruel joke to tell everyone we were making out. He says you don't like him. Which, of course, we know is the truth, but he was wrong for making it seem like you and I made out. We got into a huge fight over it and my dad had to break us up. When you gave me back the charm, I knew you were breaking up with me. I don't know if this e-mail will make you change your mind, but I ask you to give me, give us, another chance. You know how to reach me.

Marcus signed the e-mail with hearts. My heart tugged at me to call him, but maybe all of this was happening for a reason. Maybe I was too young to have a boyfriend and that's why we kept running into problems. I did know one thing. It was only a matter of time before I got DJ back. How? I hadn't determined. It was only a matter of when.

~ 30 ~

Making Up

I called Marcus back and all was forgiven. The next day I felt like I aced my test, and I danced my heart out at that night's football game. Saturday, my mom dropped me off at Jasmine's because she had a book club meeting. Jasmine got on my nerves most of the time with her snide remarks about Sierra.

"Jas, what happened? We've only been at the new school for three months and our friendship is falling apart."

"It's not me, it's Sierra. She's changed."

"You both have. I knew you could be mean and spiteful, but to your own friend?"

"Sierra can handle it."

"What about that dude you brought to homecoming? I thought you were going to kick it with him."

"How do I put this? Ian and I like the same things."

"That's a good thing."

"Not if you both like the same kind of boys."

My mouth dropped open. I never would have thought Ian was gay. "Does his dad know?"

"No, and he begged me not to tell."

"So what are you going to do?"

"It's his business. As long as he doesn't make a pass at the boys I like, we're cool."

"Thank goodness for that. I wished you would lighten up on Sierra. She hasn't been looking good these days." I still couldn't believe Ian was gay. I tried to remember if he had shown any signs at the dance. I couldn't recall. I had been too wrapped up in Marcus, and then the drama had happened.

"My parents are going to a party tonight, so why don't you ask your mom if you can stay over?" Jasmine asked, as she showed me some of her new clothes.

"I want that one." I removed the jacket from the hanger and tried it on. "I'll ask. They'll probably be glad to have some alone time."

"Your mom's pregnant, so alone time doesn't seem to be a problem."

I turned around to face Jasmine. "Speaking of my mom being pregnant, I didn't appreciate you telling everybody over at Marcus's the other weekend."

"I didn't know it was a secret or anything. Besides, soon everybody will be able to tell."

I removed the jacket and handed it to her. "Still. It's not your business to put it in the streets."

"Sorry, okay?"

"Whatever. Just be glad my mom didn't tell your mom about what you did."

Jasmine stood up and looped her arm through mine. "I've been meaning to thank you for that. I don't know what got into me. Those girls were looking at him like they wanted to jump his bones. I had to lay claim to what's mine."

"Those were his cousins."

"And their cousins' skank friends."

"Some of them were on the skanky side," I agreed.

My parents agreed that I could spend the night. We had fun watching some of our favorite movies and eating junk food. The only thing missing was Sierra. I called her a few times but her little brother informed us she wasn't able to come to the phone. I would be glad when her month's punishment came to an end.

"Girls, it's time to get up," Mrs. McNeil said the next morning, standing at the door.

I wiped the sleep from my eyes. It took me less time than Jasmine to get ready for church. She had on shades to hide her puffy eyes. I hugged my mom and dad and took a seat in the pew behind them. The cute guy that had been eyeing me for weeks walked up to me after church.

"Are you going to the youth retreat?" he asked as he handed me a flyer.

I took it and handed it to Jasmine. "I don't know. I have to ask my folks."

"I hope you do. I'll be there."

Without saying anything else, he walked away. "Girl, why didn't you tell him you had a boyfriend?"

"He was only handing me a flier."

"Playa, playa. I ain't mad atcha," Jasmine said as we walked outside to wait on our parents.

I spent a quiet Sunday afternoon with my parents. When I got tired of hanging out with them, I left them in the den and went to my room. I logged on to my computer and downloaded new music to my iPod. Marcus came online and we chatted until we both got sleepy. I was so glad we had made up.

~ 31 ~

Rock-a-Bye Baby

Monday morning came too fast for me. Marcus met me at the car. He and my mom spoke, and then I followed him into the building. I had forgotten something in my locker, so I had to make a detour. Tanisha leaned on the lockers. "Can I talk to you?"

"Good morning to you too," I said sarcastically. I looked at Marcus. "I'll see you at lunch."

"You sure?" he asked, looking at Tanisha and then back at me.

"I got this." I watched him walk away before turning around and using my hand to move Tanisha from in front of my locker. I retrieved my notebook and closed it. "What's on your mind?" I asked.

"Can you tell your friends to leave DJ alone?"

"Look Tanisha, that's between y'all."

I turned to walk away, but paused when I heard her say, "I'm pregnant." I turned to face her. "DJ's the dad but I haven't told him." By now tears were running down her face.

I didn't want her to cause a scene so I said, "Follow me." We walked to the nearest bathroom. I wet a paper towel and handed it to her.

"Sorry. I haven't told anyone and every time I get ready to tell DJ, I see one of your friends in his face."

This was more than I cared to deal with, but I kept my cool. "How far along are you?" I asked.

"I'm eight weeks."

"You need to tell him. You shouldn't be dealing with this alone."

"I've let him messages, but he won't return my calls." She started crying again.

"Confront him at lunch. If he don't want to talk to you in private, then tell it to him in front of his friends."

"But I don't want nobody to know."

"Uh I'm not a doctor or a nurse, but they'll soon know soon enough."

"Promise me you won't tell nobody."

I crossed my fingers of one hand and held it to my side. "Sure."

I couldn't believe Tanisha dropped that bombshell in my lap. I moved in slow motion and ended up tardy for class. When I saw her in the hallway later, she avoided eye contact. She pretended like we didn't have the earlier conversation, which was fine with me. DJ saw me walking in his direction and rushed inside a nearby classroom. I looked in the room as I walked by. Our eyes locked. I refused to blink. I almost bumped into someone as I kept on walking.

Tanisha stood outside the door of the cafeteria. "You going in or just blocking," I joked.

"I'm trying to get my nerves up."

"Just do it. He should have returned your call and you wouldn't have to do it here."

"You're right. Thanks, Britney." She did the unexpected and hugged me. I just stood there with my arms to my side.

She went through the door. Jasmine walked up to me. "So you're schmoozing with the enemy now."

"It's not what you think," I responded.

"Traitor."

Sierra walked up. Jasmine repeated to her what she'd seen. "I can't believe you're trying to be friends with that witch."

I ignored both of them, and hurried to get my tray so I could watch the scene I was sure would take place as soon as Tanisha told DJ her news. It didn't take her long. I heard DJ yell, "Trick, that's not my baby."

Tanisha ran past us, crying. Marcus tried to calm DJ down. He was yelling obscenities. The cafeteria monitor escorted him out. Marcus and I looked at each other. He picked up his tray and met us at our table.

Jasmine was the first to ask, "What was that all about?"

Marcus said, "Tanisha asked DJ to come talk to her. He refused, so she told him in front of all of us that he was going to be a father. That's when DJ went off."

Sierra pushed her tray away. "I've lost my appetite."

"I can't believe it," Jasmine said.

"It's true." Marcus, Jasmine, and Sierra looked in my direction. I repeated what Tanisha had told me.

"Man, that's messed up. He's in line to get a basketball scholarship. I don't know what's going to happen now," Marcus said, shaking his head.

"I feel sorry for Tanisha," I said.

"I don't. It's probably not even his baby," Sierra said.

Sierra could be so naive. Jasmine remained quiet. I hoped this made them think twice about DJ. Jasmine removed her lip gloss from her purse and applied some. "Just because she's pregnant, it doesn't mean he has to drop out."

"Babies are expensive," I said. "I should know because that's all my mom talks about lately."

"Your mom's pregnant?" Marcus asked.

"What? You didn't know? You're the only one in your family who didn't." I looked at Jasmine. Jasmine ignored me and held her mirror up so I wouldn't see her eyes.

"Another little Britney running around."

I snapped my fingers. "I'm an original."

Marcus placed his hand over mine and said, "Calm down. I thought you would be happy about a little brother or sister."

Jasmine said, "She likes being an only child."

I rolled my eyes. "Don't listen to her. I'm adjusting." I caught Jasmine making motions with her head and hands. "Anyway, this isn't about me, it's about DJ and Tanisha."

Marcus said, "DJ's dad is going to be pissed though. I'll hear what happens from DJ or my parents later."

I looked back and forth between Sierra and Jasmine. "Which one of you want to be the step-mama?" I laughed.

"I don't find it funny," Jasmine said, standing up. "I'm out of here."

"Don't go, Jas. Can't you take a joke?" I teased.

Sierra remained quiet throughout the conversation. She looked worried. Something was going on with her, but with Marcus there, I wouldn't be able to find out now. The bell rang. I had barely touched my food. Marcus took my tray and dumped it for me. "I need to go find out what's going on with DJ or else I'd walk you to class," he said.

Although I didn't like DJ, I understood he was his cousin, so I didn't trip.

~ 32 ~

A Close Call

Marcus called me later and gave me an update on DJ and Tanisha's situation. Sierra was off punishment so I couldn't wait to do a three-way conference call with her and Jasmine. Once we were all connected, I said, "DJ's parents and Tanisha's mother are supposed to meet up so they can discuss the baby."

Sierra said, "I wonder how DJ is. He didn't return any of my calls."

I rolled my eyes as if she could see me, and then leaned back on the bed and continued to talk. "So now will you two stop acting a fool over the dude?"

"He needs to get a blood test. The baby might not even be his." Jasmine popped a bubble in our ears.

"Tanisha said he's the father of the baby and I believe her." I was so wrapped up in my phone conversation that I didn't hear my mom walk in. She cleared her throat a few times. I opened up my eyes and sat straight up. I hoped she hadn't overheard my conversation. "I'll see y'all tomorrow." They protested, but I hung up anyway.

My mom sat on the edge of my bed and confirmed my fears. "I didn't mean to eavesdrop, but I'm glad I did come in. We need to talk."

"Tanisha's this girl at school. She's a sophomore."

"And pregnant," my mom filled in the blanks.

"I felt bad for her. She was crying and the father of the baby acted like she was lying."

"That's how boys will do you. They know they're the only one you're sleeping with, but let you get pregnant and *bam*. They'll swear up and down they're not the daddy."

"I don't like the baby's daddy anyway."

"Lord, I hope I never have to hear you say somebody's your baby daddy," she said with a worried look on her face.

I hoped not either. "You don't have to worry about that with me, Mom. I'm not doing anything."

"If you do decide to do something, promise me you'll come and talk to me first." I didn't say anything, so she repeated herself. "Promise me, Britney."

"Yes, Mom. I'll come to you first."

"I hope this is a lesson to you to be careful. It's best to wait until you're married to have kids. That's what me and your father did and I'm glad we did."

I listened to her go down memory lane about how she and my dad had been college sweethearts, broke up shortly after graduation but reconnected after running into each other after one of his concerts. Their story was forever etched in my mind.

It didn't take me long to drift off to sleep after my mom left, but my cell phone beeped and woke me up again. It was a message from Marcus wishing me a good night. I tossed the phone on the other side of the bed, and went back to sleep.

The next day, rumors were flying all over school about Tanisha and DJ. Tanisha wasn't in school, but DJ was, and he walked around like nothing had happened. Somebody needed to knock the smug look off his face. Rumor had it that Tanisha would now have to go to school somewhere else, because our school didn't allow pregnant girls to attend; it could be disruptive to classes.

I had to walk by DJ and his crew of friends to get to one of my classes. I hoped Marcus was in the crew, but I didn't see him. I heard a couple of whistles. I refused to acknowledge them. DJ said, "She's so stuck up, I don't see what my cuz sees in her."

Someone said, "Man, she's a dime. If he wasn't with her, I would push up on that."

I just rolled my eyes and kept on walking. After school I met up with Sierra and Jasmine. "Did you hear that Tanisha got kicked out of school?" Jasmine asked.

"You should be happy. She was your worst enemy," I responded.

"But to be kicked out of school because she's pregnant. That's messed up."

Sierra said, "She should have used birth control."

I repeated to them some of the things my mom had told me. "Birth control doesn't guarantee that you won't get pregnant. According to my mom, that's the mistake a lot of girls make."

"I know I'm not doing it until I'm good and ready," Jasmine said, as she waved at her sister waiting for her.

Sierra asked, "Can you get pregnant if you let him rub you?"

Jasmine and I both stopped walking. We moved in closer. I said, "Don't tell me you let DJ."

"Oh my God," Jasmine yelled.

A few people walking by stopped to look in our direction. Jasmine's sister called out her name. She yelled, "Give me a minute."

"The night of the dance. DJ touched me down there."

"And you're just now telling us. You mean with the same hand he uses to hold my hand? How disgusting," Jasmine said.

"You don't have to tell everybody," Sierra responded.

"I swear you two are like a Jerry Springer episode," I stated.

Brenda walked up to where we were standing. "Jas, unless you want to walk home, I suggest you get your butt to the car. Britney, I saw your mama waiting over there." She pointed to the left of where we stood.

"Sierra, call me later." I couldn't wait to hear the rest of the story. I asked my mom as soon as I got in the car, "Can you get pregnant if a boy rubs you down there?"

I thought my mom was going to have a wreck. She stopped abruptly. "Are you and Marcus doing things I should know about?"

"No, Mom. Please. One of the girls at school was concerned after hearing about Tanisha being pregnant."

My mom pulled over into a parking lot. "The best thing for you to do is to not do anything and you won't have to worry about that."

"I know. I don't plan on doing anything. I mean, kissing is enough." I let that slip.

"What do you know about kissing?" she asked.

"Nothing. I'm just saying. To me kissing is enough. I wouldn't even think about doing those other things."

"Letting boys rub and touch here and there could lead to other things, and before you know it you're having sex and ending up pregnant or catching a disease."

"What do I tell the girl at school?"

"Tell her that she shouldn't let the guy rub her like that anymore."

"So she's probably not pregnant." Sierra would be relieved.

~ 33 ~

Can You Stand the Rain?

"**I**f it ain't Miss 'She thinks she's all that'," DJ's voice rang from behind me. I was putting things in my locker before heading to dance rehearsal.

I ignored him until I could feel his hot breath on the back of my neck as he placed one arm on the locker. I looked him in the eyes. "You might want to move." I didn't need an excuse to hit him.

"You got my cousin fooled, but I know you really want to get with me. You can't stand the fact I'm talking to your friends."

"You're a jerk and I don't know what any girl sees in you."

"You want me and I'll prove it." Before I could react, DJ bent down and kissed me. I slapped him and pushed him away. I wiped my mouth. He started laughing. "I knew it. You want me."

"I'm telling Marcus," I said, as I stormed away, bumping right into Marcus.

Marcus's eyes looked cold. "I saw it all for myself."

If he had, why did he seem angry with me? "You need to do something about your cousin," I said.

"He told me he could get you to kiss him. For once he wasn't lying," Marcus said.

What? I know he doesn't think I kissed him voluntarily. "Marcus, if you saw everything, it's clear that he forced himself on me."

"From where I was standing you didn't seem to protest."

I was livid. "You can't say that. I pushed him away and slapped him." I couldn't get my words out right.

"But why did it take you so long to get out of his face? I saw everything."

Sierra called my name out. "Ms. Albright's about to start."

I picked up my backpack that had fallen to the side and placed it on my back. "Marcus, we can discuss this later. I got to go."

Marcus made me mad because he wanted to believe what DJ said. I wasn't going give an apology for something I didn't do. If he expected one, he would be waiting until Michael Jordan returned to the NBA.

I missed several moves during rehearsal. Ms. Albright reprimanded me in front of the team. I felt embarrassed, but I knew why I was out of sync. I checked my cell phone to see if I had any messages after rehearsal, but there were none. I guessed Marcus didn't want to talk to me.

I told Sierra what had happened with DJ earlier, as we waited on my mom to pick us up. "I don't believe you," Sierra responded.

"I have no reason to lie about it," I insisted.

"You keep trying to make DJ out to be some type of monster, but I'm beginning to think you really do want him for yourself."

Oh, no, she didn't. My mom pulled up before I could tell Sierra off. "Let's table it until later," I said.

"As far as I'm concerned this conversation is over."

"Fine." I opened up the front door of the car and got in.

Sierra and I barely opened our mouths. "Rehearsal that bad?" my mom probed.

I mumbled, "Ask her," under my breath.

My mom didn't push any further. She turned the volume up on the radio, and we rode with loud music playing until we dropped Sierra off at home. As soon as she was out of the car, my mom bombarded me with questions.

"Mom, I don't know what else to do. I've done

everything I can think of to show them DJ is no good."

"Then stop. Don't do anything."

"I'm losing my two best friends because of him. I might even lose Marcus because of him," I confessed.

"Britney, you know I like Marcus, but you don't need to be too serious with one guy now anyway. You have more than three years of high school left."

"I know, but I really like Marcus."

"Just make sure whatever it is you're dealing with, it doesn't interfere with your grades." She sounded like she knew I wasn't telling her everything. She was right. There was more to it, but I couldn't let her know about DJ kissing me.

Marcus didn't call me that night and I refused to call him. I checked my e-mail the next morning. I sorted it by name, but there weren't any messages from Marcus. I was so upset that I forgot to put on any lip gloss. Jasmine was the one who pointed it out to me when she saw me as I walked towards the school's entrance.

"You need to borrow my lip gloss," she said as she handed me an unopened tube.

I had some of my own, but I liked grape, so I took it. Nothing like a new tube of lip gloss to cheer me up.

~ 34 ~

Easier Said

"Sierra's not talking to me, so what's up with her these days?" Jasmine said.

"This time she's mad at me."

Jasmine and I talked as we walked to homeroom. "Promise me you won't get mad too," I said.

"What did you do?"

I explained to her what had happened the day before with DJ. Jasmine's reaction didn't mimic Sierra's; instead, she got upset at DJ. "Wait until I see him."

I attempted to calm her down. "Don't cause a scene. It was bad enough dealing with Marcus afterwards."

"If you want me to, I'll talk to Marcus." That was the first kind gesture Jasmine had made toward me in a while.

"Forget Marcus," I said, still upset that I hadn't heard from him.

"There he goes now." She pointed down the hall.

I hoped he didn't see me. Unfortunately, he did. Instead of walking toward us though, he turned and walked the other way. "Did you see that?" I asked.

"I'll go talk to him," she said.

"No," I said, but Jasmine ignored me and continued on her quest to talk to Marcus. I walked toward our class. Sierra sat in her normal seat, but didn't look up when I entered. I ignored her too.

I listened to my iPod as I waited for class to start. Jasmine barely made it to class before the last tardy bell rang. She mouthed the words, "I'll write you," as she took her seat. When the teacher wasn't looking, Jasmine had someone pass me a note. I had to wait another five minutes before getting a chance to read it.

Her note said, "Marcus said he's not mad at you, but just needs some time to think."

I looked in Jasmine's direction. She shrugged her shoulders. I folded the letter up and put it in my notebook. I would make the decision for Marcus. We were through. Like my mom said, I was too young to be committed to one boy anyway. I wished my heart agreed. Maybe the pain would go away if it did. I felt like crying, but knew now was not the time. I did my best to concentrate in my classes, but it was hard.

Jasmine and I waited outside the cafeteria door for Sierra, but she didn't come. We got our food and took a seat at our normal table. While we were eating, Sierra appeared. Instead of heading to our table, she took a seat where DJ, Marcus, and their friends were sitting. "Did she just roll her eyes at me?" Jasmine asked.

"Let it go," I responded. I noticed that Sierra had rolled her eyes too, but I was dealing with enough drama.

"DJ's been avoiding me all day, but I'm going to catch his butt after lunch and tell him a thing or two," Jasmine insisted.

"Drop it, okay? Marcus and I are through and there's nothing you or anyone else can do about it." My eyes watered. I picked up a napkin and pretended like something was in my eyes and wiped them.

"Girl, don't be crying over no boy. You don't see me crying over DJ, do you?" Jasmine pretended to be so hard, but I could see through the façade.

"So you finally admit DJ is no good." I drank the juice, but barely touched my food.

"I've always known he wasn't any good, but what can I say. I like the bad boys." She wiped her mouth with her napkin. She picked up her makeup mirror and applied a coat of lip gloss.

"We need to get Sierra away from him before he does something," I said.

"Sierra's old enough to know better," Jasmine responded.

Jasmine had a point. She reminded me of what my mom had said a few days earlier. I need to just step aside and let what was going to happen happen. For me, it was easier said than done. I was doing my best not to get obsessed with finding a way to get back at DJ.

Sierra's attitude carried over into dance rehearsal. Normally we practiced near each other, but on this day, she made it a point to go sit near Nikki, the leader of our dance squad. I tried to catch up with her after dance, but she avoided me. We were riding home together, so she couldn't avoid me forever.

When I made it outside, I saw her getting in a strange vehicle. I saw my mom and walked to the car. "Where's Sierra going?" she asked after I got in.

"I don't know. She's not talking to me."

"She's still tripping over a guy."

"Yep," I responded.

"I try not to interfere with you girls' squabbles, but this has gone on long enough. I'll talk to her mom about this later."

Normally, I would have begged for my mom not to say anything, but Sierra deserved whatever backlash would come from it. Somebody had to make her see it was a huge mistake to put so much trust in a guy who didn't have her best interest at heart.

When I got home, I called Jasmine and told her about the conversation I'd had with my mom. "Sierra's going to be mad at you," Jasmine said.

"So what? It's not like she's talking to me now anyway."

I logged on to my computer and saw Sierra online. She logged off a few minutes after I connected. *I guess she thought I was going to send her an instant message. I didn't want to talk to her anyway.* I continued to talk to Jasmine. I needed to do some research for a paper, so I soon hung up with her. It didn't take me long to discover the information I needed. I printed out a few sheets and took the rest of the night writing my paper. It wasn't due until the end of the week, but I was glad to have finished so I wouldn't have to worry about it.

My dad was out of town and I missed him. He was busy but I wished he were there. I sent him a quick text message, and he responded, letting me know he was thinking about me too. We exchanged a few more text messages and then he had to get back to his meeting. He promised to call me before school tomorrow. With all that was going on, at least I could count on my daddy's love.

~ 35 ~

Moving Right Along

"Mama, can I go to the youth retreat at church?" I asked before exiting the car the next day.

"When is it?"

I pulled out the flyer from my backpack and handed it to her. "It's the weekend of Halloween."

"Sure. That'll be good. Is Jasmine or Sierra going?" she asked.

"I'm not sure. To be honest, I want to go regardless if they go or not."

"Good deal. Let me make sure your dad doesn't have something planned for that weekend; otherwise, you can go."

"Cool." I reached over and hugged her as best I could with us both sitting in the front seat.

Sierra stood talking to DJ and Marcus. Marcus angled his body so his back was toward me. I walked past them without speaking. Jasmine sat on a concrete bench near the front stairs. She stood up as soon as she saw me.

"What's up? You see Ms. Traitor."

I looked in the direction of where I had last seen Sierra standing. They were all walking our way. "She'll be changing her tune as soon as her mom hears about everything."

Jasmine moved to stand in front of DJ. I tried to stop her, but failed. "Oh, you think you're something, you lying bastard."

"Jas, move out my way before I hurt you girl," DJ said. He stopped and everyone walking with him stopped too.

"You're a low-down dirty dog, making a pass at your cousin's woman. You're disgusting."

"I said move, girl."

Jasmine moved from in front of him and stood in front of Sierra. "You're so blind you can't see he's playing you. He couldn't sleep with me so now he's trying to get in your panties."

"Jas, that's enough. Come on," I said, grabbing her by the arm.

"That's right, you better get your girl," DJ said.

I stopped. I let go of Jasmine's arm and turned around. "Don't say anything to me because I'm this close," I used my hand to illustrate, "from going up-side your head."

He moved toward me. I didn't move. "I wish you would."

I moved closer to him, but Marcus ran and jumped between us. I said, "I'm not scared of you. Just because I'm a girl don't mean I won't commence to beating the crap out of you."

Jasmine stood on the sidelines applauding me. Sierra held her head down low. DJ wrapped his arm around Sierra and said, "Come on, baby. These chicks ain't your friends. If they were, they wouldn't be hating on what you and I have."

Sierra looked back at us as they all walked away. I could tell Jasmine was still upset because I had to almost run to keep up with her pace. "That Sierra is one dumb chick," Jasmine said.

"Just a few days ago, you were acting the same way over DJ," I commented.

"Never."

Yeah, right. Jasmine didn't want to admit it, but up until recently, she'd acted the same way Sierra had with DJ; to a point that now our three-best-friend friendship was no longer intact. First, Sierra was mad at Jasmine, but now I was included because she believed whatever crap DJ had been feeding her.

I changed the subject as we walked to homeroom.

"My mom said I could go to the youth retreat at church, so I'm going to that."

"Ooh, and see that cute guy from church, too. You go, girl."

"I'm not going for him. I do have a boyfriend."

"Marcus is not speaking to you, so in my book he's been downgraded to ex."

She had a point. There's no relationship if two people couldn't talk to each other. As much as I hated to believe it, Marcus and I were through. He had broken up with me over something he thought he saw. DJ probably didn't make the situation better with the things he said. If Marcus would let his cousin break us up, then so be it. I was going to move on. I wasn't moving on to be with the guy at church, but I refused to shed another tear over Marcus Johnson.

I was in my own little world while walking to one of my classes when I heard Marcus say, "Sorry about what happened earlier."

"No biggie. I'm a big girl. I can take care of myself."

"Just checking to make sure everything's all right."

"It's all good."

"See you later," he responded.

I watched him walk to his class. I wondered what that was all about. Boys' actions confused me, but moving right along.

~ 36 ~

The Retreat

Jasmine and I decided to attend the youth retreat at church. She was the first person I saw when my dad and I pulled up. "Call me when you're ready for me to pick you up," my dad said.

"It's supposed to be over at ten," I responded as I exited the car.

Jasmine and I both waved at my dad. Jasmine said, "Girl, this is going to be exciting. I saw the cute guy and some more guys inside."

"I told you, I'm here to have a good time. I could care less about any of the boys."

Jasmine ignored me. "Come on. Let's go so we can get a good seat."

One of the coordinators had us pull numbers and separated us into different groups. I was disappointed that Jasmine and I got separated. There were about fifty kids, so we were divided into five groups. "This is a way for you to get to know other members of the church. Not just your friends or relatives."

The cute guy was in the group with Jasmine. She smiled. I didn't. We introduced ourselves to each other. One of the coordinators handed out some papers for the first competition. "The first group to name the most books of the Bible will win some free movie tickets," said a petite woman wearing a baseball cap.

This was going to be fun. I wanted those movie tickets, so I hoped my team members knew their books. The game was like Jeopardy. We came in second place so we didn't win anything. Jasmine's team won. We did win one of the games and got gift cards to a local bookstore. There was enough on the card for me to buy one of the latest teen books, so I was happy.

Later on, we put together bags to give out to the little kids who would be coming for their Halloween party. It was fun passing them out to the kids. The cute guy (as he had become known to me and Jasmine) was actually named Travis Edwards. He went to Mesquite High School, another school in the Dallas Metroplex.

"Can I get your number and call you sometime?" he asked as we passed out the last treats to the kids.

"I'll think about it." I walked away to see if he would come after me. He did.

"I'll be getting a car next year."

"You don't have to try to impress me," I said.

"So what's it gonna be?"

"I don't have a pen."

He pulled out a pen from his pocket and picked up a napkin from a nearby table. He handed them both to me. I wrote down my cell phone number and e-mail address. "Don't lose it." I handed it back to him and walked to where Jasmine stood.

I had a huge grin on my face. Jasmine winked at me. "I got a few numbers myself," she said, as she scrolled through her cell phone.

"I'm glad I decided to come."

"Me too. Forget Marcus and DJ."

We high-fived each other. We ate pizza and the retreat ended. Overall, I had a good time. I didn't think about Marcus once. *Okay, maybe once.* I turned my cell phone back on to find out where my dad was. He happened to already be outside. "See y'all later," I said to Jasmine and the other teens I had bonded with during the retreat. I hugged the advisors.

"Did you enjoy yourself, sweetheart?" my dad asked.

"I had so much fun. I can't wait until the next one."
I buckled my seatbelt.

"Good. Your mom was telling me things were getting too serious with you and that Marcus guy."

"Dad."

"Don't 'Dad' me. I think you need to cool it with him anyway."

"I thought you liked Marcus."

"I do, but you're still too young to be having a boyfriend."

"I'm fourteen now."

"And what does that mean to me?"

"Girls are getting pregnant at fifteen these days," I said before I caught myself. That argument was the wrong thing to bring up.

"That's why I shouldn't be letting you date until you're thirty."

I didn't immediately see the smile on his face. He continued to say, "Just kidding. But seriously, you're too young. I hope you don't make the same mistake as some of these other hot girls I see out there. Like your friend Jasmine. Dion need to rein her in before she gets out of control."

"Jas isn't fast."

"I couldn't tell from the way she acted last month. I'm just saying. If you think me or your mom would disapprove, don't do it."

I folded my arms and eased back in my seat. The leather seemed to wrap around me. I didn't want to be having this conversation with my dad. I changed the subject to something else he enjoyed talking about: music.

~ 37 ~

Missed Call

Marcus continued to go out of his way to avoid me at school. His actions bothered me, but as the week went by I stopped caring as much. I hadn't heard from Travis yet, and I was okay with it. What I wasn't feeling was the tension that surrounded my friendship with Sierra. Jasmine and I were back to talking, but it was a little strained when I brought up Sierra.

Jasmine could hold a grudge. She was still mad at her about DJ. She figured she went out with him first, so Sierra should have backed off. I tried to convince her they both were wrong for going after the same guy in the first place. She refused to see her part in the tension in our three-way friendship.

"Look at her. She's wearing his jacket," Jasmine said as she looked in Sierra's direction.

I refused to look. "Like my grandmamma would say, if she likes it, I love it."

"Here she comes." Jasmine turned around and pretended as if we were in a deep conversation.

"Do you mind if I sit here?" Sierra asked.

Jasmine looked at me. I looked at her. Jasmine shook her head no. I spoke out loud, "No."

She sat down and started talking as if it were old times. Jasmine and I remained quiet as we listened to her gossip about other people in school. I didn't know about Jasmine, but I was getting tired of listening. I looked at my watch. "I'm going to be late for class, so I'll catch y'all later."

"I'm right behind you," Jasmine said.

We left Sierra sitting at our table. When we were outside of the cafeteria, I said, "Can you believe Sierra? I don't know what her problem is."

"I do and it has two initials," Jasmine responded.

"Girl, I rushed out of there so fast I forgot to put on some more lip gloss."

"Me too."

We took a detour to the bathroom. We were laughing at something crazy Jasmine had said, when we exited and ran right into Sierra. She'd gotten her man, but she didn't look too happy. "You should find an available stall because nobody else was in there," I said without stopping to talk to her.

Jasmine and I separated, and I walked past Marcus talking to the same girl he'd been talking to outside of my gym class about a month ago. He put his arm around her. *I guess I'm supposed to be jealous.* His little move backfired though, because I walked by them as if I didn't see them. I was concentrating so hard on not looking back at Marcus that when I bumped into DJ, it startled me.

"Watch where you're going!" he yelled.

"You the one need to watch it."

"Don't be bitter 'cause your man is talking to another girl."

"He can talk to whoever he wants. We're no longer together, but I'm not telling you something you didn't know." I had one hand on my hip and rolled my neck.

One of the hall monitors walked up. "Is everything okay over there?" he asked.

"Fine. I was just going to class." I left DJ standing there.

Sierra went out of her way after rehearsal to hold a long conversation. Since she had been acting funny with me, I had my mom pick me up and told her I thought it was best to have Sierra's mom pick her up from now on. "Let's cut the bull," I said, facing Sierra in the school entrance door. We waited there because it was a little cool outside and neither one of our mothers had pulled up yet.

"I know things haven't been so cool with us lately," Sierra admitted.

"It's your fault."

"I'm sorry, okay? Is that what you wanted to hear? I'm sorry. I miss my friends. DJ and his friends are okay, but I miss y'all."

Any sympathy I was feeling towards Sierra vanished at the mention of DJ's name. "You made your choice. You've shown where your loyalty lies."

"Come on now. We're in high school. We should be able to have different sets of friends."

I laughed. "Nobody's trying to control who you be friends with."

"I can't tell. You're worse than Jasmine. Just because you don't like DJ, it doesn't mean I have to not like him."

"Here we go again. For a straight-A student, you can be so stupid."

Sierra started crying. I wanted to reach out to her but she made me mad. My mom happened to pull up in front of the building, so I left her standing there with her thoughts and tears.

I didn't say much on the ride home. I picked over my food at dinner. Ms. Pearl complained about it when I took my dishes to the kitchen. "What's wrong?" she asked.

"Sierra's been acting funny and today she reached out to me and I made her cry." I told her about the situation, leaving out certain parts.

"Looks to me like you girls are growing up and growing apart. Everything has a season. Maybe the season for your friendship has passed," Ms. Pearl said.

I didn't want to believe it, but there could have been some truth in what she was saying. What else could explain the craziness? Ms. Pearl went on to say, "Then again, maybe Sierra is trying to find herself. During this discovery she's lashing out at the people who mean the most to her."

Ms. Pearl's words of wisdom confused me. I left the kitchen more puzzled than ever. My phone was beeping when I entered my bedroom. I removed it from the charger. I had several missed calls. One was from a number I didn't recognize. I hoped it was the call I had been waiting on. There was only one way to find out, and that was to check my new messages.

I jumped up and down when I heard Travis's voice in my voice mail. He left me his phone number. I didn't bother to listen to my other messages. I clicked off the phone, got comfortable, and then called Travis.

He sounded so cute. Our conversation didn't last too long because his older brother kept picking up. "I'll call you later."

I saved his number in my phone. I called Jasmine afterwards to tell her he'd called. "So what are you going to do about Marcus?" she asked.

"Marcus who?" I laughed.

It was cheesy the way things ended with me and Marcus, but it was obvious he had moved on without caring about my feelings, so I would do the same. I had a few low grades I needed to bring up before the end of the semester. I wasn't going to let Marcus or any other guy interfere with my school work ever again.

~ 38 ~

Turkey Day

The school was having a day where parents could come and have lunch with their kids. From what I understood, they did it every year right before Thanksgiving. Today was the day. It was cool, so instead of a skirt uniform, I opted to wear pants and the new leather jacket I had gotten from the mall the week before.

"I promise to be there at eleven sharp," my dad said as I kissed him on the cheek.

"If you're late, I'll save you a plate." I followed my mom out the door. "I wished you would come too," I said to her as we got in the car.

"My stomach is a little sensitive these days. Something tells me your school cafeteria's food wouldn't sit well with me."

I had to agree with her. Half the time *I* didn't want to eat the food. I had planned on bringing my lunch, but it was just easier to attempt to eat whatever they served; at least until I could get my own car. I thumbed through one of the gossip magazines while she drove me to school. Marcus waited for me by the curb. "Hi, Mrs. Franklin."

"Hey, Marcus. How are your folks doing?"

"They're doing fine," he responded.

"Tell your mom I said hi," my mom said before pulling away.

"What do you want, Marcus?" I asked as I headed up the walkway.

"I wanted to say I forgive you."

I stopped. I looked him up and down. "Oh, no you didn't. I haven't done anything to be forgiven for."

"You kissed DJ."

"News flash: DJ forced himself on me, so he is the one who should be apologizing."

I walked away. He reached for my arm. I turned around. "What now?"

"Can we start over?"

"Go start over with Marie. She's the one I've been seeing you walking with."

He said something but, I don't know what, because I ran into the school. Forget Marcus. Now that I had gotten him out of my system, he wanted to weasel his way back in my life. Nope. That wasn't going to happen.

At lunchtime I waited near the office so I could meet my dad. Marcus walked up to me. "About this morning. I'm sorry," he said.

"It's already been forgotten," I replied.

My dad snuck up on me. "Hey, baby girl," he said as he hugged me. "What's up, Marcus?"

"Hi, Mr. Franklin," he responded.

"Come on, Dad. I want you to meet some of my teachers." I took his hand and introduced him around the room. Afterward, I led him into the cafeteria. "Now you'll get to see what I have to put up with every day."

"The food can't be that bad," my dad said.

The cafeteria workers were friendlier than usual and the room was decorated to fit the Thanksgiving holiday. "I think she likes you," I teased, as the server piled two scoops of dressing onto my dad's plate.

He paid for our meals. I looked in the direction of where I regularly sat. Jasmine waved her arm in the air to get my attention. Her mom had come and was seated next to her. When we reached the table, they both stood up and hugged my dad. Mrs. McNeil's blouse was too tight and too low-cut. Her attempt to hold on to her youth was failing in my opinion. Of course, I would never say to Jasmine what I was thinking.

"Dion tells me you guys might be going to Aspen for Thanksgiving," Mrs. McNeil said in between bites.

"We were thinking about it. We wanted to take one more trip before the baby comes."

Why is this the first time I'm hearing about this trip? I would rather go somewhere warmer like Miami.

"Destiny's about four or five months pregnant now, isn't she?"

"Yes, and it's been hell on all of us since she found out," he joked.

"I remember those strange cravings. I used to have Dion go out and get me pickles and orange juice."

Jasmine and I both made faces as if we wanted to puke. Those two things didn't seem too appetizing. Lunch went by fast. Several of the kids made comments as they passed by. No matter how low-key my dad tried to be, someone always recognized him.

By the time we exited the cafeteria, some folks from the media were waiting. All we saw were flashes. A few stuck microphones in his face. "Is this the first time you've been to your daughter's school?"

"Please give us some privacy."

"Why isn't she in private school?" The questions kept coming. My dad held my hand and we pushed past the reporters. "Sorry, Bri, for the interruptions."

I hugged him. "At least we had a quiet lunch."

"Get to class and let me go handle the vultures . . . I mean, media."

I watched my dad put on his game face. He handled those reporters like a pro. "Girl, your dad is so fine," one of the girls in my next class said when she passed me.

"He sure is," another girl said.

I pretended to ignore them, but I heard every word they said. *If this is what my mom had to go through, I could understand why she ended up in some of the fights I used to hear them talk about.*

Ms. Albright cut dance rehearsal short. "We won't have rehearsal during the holidays, but that doesn't mean you're not to practice the routines."

Several of us started talking amongst ourselves. She tapped her foot. "Have a good Thanksgiving and don't eat too much."

"What are you doing for Thanksgiving?" Sierra asked, as we walked back to the dressing room to change our outfits. "My mom has some family coming in from out of town. I was going to ask if you wanted to come over."

"If we don't go to Aspen, we'll be going to Louisiana.

My grandparents stay in Shreveport and we haven't seen them in a while."

"Oh, I understand."

I was curious, so I asked, "Is DJ going to be there?"

She looked away. "Uh, I don't know. He's supposed to be." She didn't seem too confident that he would be. Knowing her dad, there was no way I could see him allowing the dude to come over to visit with his daughter; but then again I never thought our friendship would be strained, either.

~ 39 ~

Winter Wonderland

Travis called me several times over the Thanksgiving holiday. Marcus had left me a few messages too, but I didn't return any of his calls. I was surprised my cell phone picked up a signal in the mountains. My mom's belly stuck out and she looked like a little butterball dressed up in her snow bunny outfit. I couldn't understand why she wanted to come to a ski resort when her condition prevented her from skiing. This was our third day and I was bored. "Mom, can I get some skiing lessons?"

"Oh, no. I thought skiing was for white folks." She tried to mimic me.

I rolled my eyes. "You were right. Skiing is for anybody who wants to learn." She got up from her stool and wrapped her arms around me.

"That's all I was trying to get you to see." She went to her purse and handed me some money. "I expect you back in two hours."

I kissed her on the cheek. I signed up for a lesson. None of the people on the slopes looked like us, but I wasn't going to let that deter me from learning how to ski. I saw my dad in the distance talking to a group of men. He seemed comfortable around them. He looked over in my direction. I waved. He waved back.

I fell a few times, but it was fun learning how to ski. I wanted to try my hand at another slope, but the instructor didn't think I was ready. I had some time to spare, so I walked over to another slope and watched some of the skiers.

"Pretty, isn't it?" my dad asked as he took a seat next to me.

"Yes. I feel so relaxed out here."

We watched a few more skiers. "We better get going so your mama won't send a posse out to look for us."

I brushed some of the snow off me and followed my dad up the hill to our cabin. The heat hitting my face when he opened the door felt good. I removed my snow gear and stood by the fireplace to warm up.

'Hey, stop that," I said, as I caught my folks kissing in the kitchen.

My mom removed herself from my father's embrace, and grabbed a tray of food. "Teddy, get that other tray. Bri, grab the pitcher out of the fridge."

"Happy Thanksgiving. Next year this time we'll be sharing it with our new family members." Both of my parents looked at me. Mom continued, "Bri. We're having twins."

I dropped my fork and it hit the edge of the plate before falling on the table. My mouth dropped open. "Tell me this is a joke. Where are the hidden cameras?" I looked around.

My dad said, "Baby girl, we're having twins. Right now we don't know if they're going to be boys or girls. We're hoping for one of each."

"You picked a fine time to tell me." I pushed away from the table. I searched for my coat.

"Let her be. She'll be okay," my mom said.

"She has to learn she can't walk away every time she hears something she doesn't like."

This time my father won the argument, because he blocked the doorway so I couldn't leave. "Have a seat, young lady."

I took my time, but sat down on the sofa. I crossed my arms. I looked at the floor. He sat next to me. "The babies will be here before you know it, so you have two choices: Deal with it or deal with it."

If he was trying to be funny, he didn't succeed. I

couldn't see any humor in our situation. "We're getting a nanny so it's not like you'll have to take care of them, but we do expect you to spend time with them and love them. Is that understood?"

I mumbled, "Yes, sir."

"I can't hear you."

I repeated myself. I thought about what he said. If they were hiring a nanny, then maybe my life wouldn't be disrupted too much. He had given me something to think about.

"You'll always be my baby girl," he said, and squeezed my hand.

I hated to admit it, but I was a daddy's girl.

"Come on. Your mom's ready for dessert."

I followed him back to the dining room. "I'm sorry, Mom." I reached around the chair and hugged her.

That night I shared with Jasmine the news about the twins. She couldn't believe it either. We went back and forth with ways that my mom having babies might change my life. So Sierra wouldn't hear about it from someone else, I sent her a text message. Less than a minute later, she responded. We went back and forth texting one another. I asked her about her Thanksgiving. She responded that DJ hadn't shown up. I sent a quick "I'm sorry," and ended our texting session.

~ 40 ~

Sweet December

Travis asked me about being his girlfriend, but I didn't think it was a good idea. I could tell he was disappointed, but after dealing with Marcus, I wanted to chill when it came to boyfriends. Unlike Marcus, Travis seemed to understand me. He accepted our friendship and continued to call on a regular basis.

"You're wrong for leading him on," Jasmine said.

"I've told him how I felt. He knows I'm not looking for a boyfriend."

"Still. You let him leave those comments on your MySpace page. And what about the cards he mails you?"

"There's nothing wrong with that."

"Well, Brenda said be careful who you accept gifts from."

"He's only buying me cards."

"I bet you he gets you something for Christmas."

"I don't know. We haven't talked about it." Jasmine was irritating me. The way she acted, you would have thought she was Travis's friend instead of mine. Since she was all up in my business, I stated, "I haven't heard you talk about anyone recently."

She tilted her head to the side. "There's nobody to talk about. Most of the guys around here are lame."

Before I could finish asking her questions, Sierra stopped at the table. "How much are we spending on gifts this year?"

I didn't know about Jasmine, but Sierra's question caught me off guard. I started to respond, "I didn't know we were exchanging gifts," but I kept quiet.

DJ came over. "Sierra, I need to talk to you."

"Can't you see we were talking?" Jasmine responded.

"Trick, I wasn't talking to you."

Jasmine pushed her chair back and it fell to the floor. People around the cafeteria started looking in our direction. "I'll go. Jas, chill out."

Marcus picked up her chair and pushed it close to her. "Your boy wants a butt whooping from me," Jasmine said. Her hands were shaking.

"I've missed you," Marcus said, as he took a seat at our table.

"I'm a third wheel, so I'm bouncing," Jasmine said.

"Jas, stay. Whatever Marcus has to say, he can say in front of you."

"Will you give us another chance?"

Jasmine intervened. "Let me answer it for you." She looked at Marcus. "Are you ready to admit DJ is a liar and you shouldn't have been tripping with my girl over his lie?"

Jasmine had a point. I wanted to know the answer to the question myself. Marcus said, "If it'll get me my girl back, then yes."

Jasmine looked at me. "Bri, do you accept his apology?"

"Maybe."

"Will you be my girl again? Please."

"Please don't beg. Didn't someone teach you girls don't like wimps," Jasmine said.

I tried my best not to laugh. "Jas, I got it from here. I'll see you later."

Jasmine left us at the table. I lowered my voice because I didn't like folks in my business. "Marcus, it's been almost two months since that DJ thing and I just can't see going backward. I like you, but I have to think about me."

"Bri, I never stopped loving you."

"Answer this: Why were you so quick to believe what DJ said?"

"He's my cousin. We're blood. Girls lie."

I reached out for his hand and held it. "Remember when we first met and you asked me if I was using you to get to DJ?" He shook his head up and down. "What answer did I give you?"

He thought about it for a minute and responded, "You said if you wanted DJ, you wouldn't have been there with me."

"Exactly. So why would you believe him? It's obvious he's jealous of you. Obvious to me anyway."

"Bri, I'm sorry. If I have to spend the rest of the school year showing you that, I will."

I removed my hand from on top of his. "Well you might get tired because that's exactly what you will have to do. When or if I ever decide to be your girlfriend, it'll be on my terms." I left him at the table to think about what I'd said.

I felt confident. *Would I ever take Marcus back? Maybe. Maybe not.* It was December and I had several tests I needed to concentrate on. I wanted a good grade point average for my first semester. Dealing with the twins was all the drama I could stand. I didn't need any boy drama.

~ 41 ~

Give Me an A

My mom's stomach seemed to balloon overnight. She looked like she was nine months pregnant and had about three more months to go. "I might have to hire you a driver," she said, as she struggled to get behind the wheel.

"Ooh that would be cool."

She laughed. "I knew you would like that."

My mom liked to listen to the *Tom Joyner Morning Show*, so we listened to it on the ride to school. "I have something for you," she said. She reached into her purse and handed me a small gift bag.

I loved getting presents so I didn't wait to open it. It was three tickets to *High School Musical*. "Mama, you're the greatest." I hugged her and tried not to hurt her stomach.

"You've been moping around the house for the past few days, so I thought that would cheer you up."

I couldn't wait to tell Jasmine and Sierra about our front row seats. There was still tension between us all, but if Sierra didn't want to go, I could always ask one of the girls from church. My mom didn't have to worry about the third ticket going to waste. I breezed through the day thinking about the performance. I hoped we got to meet some of the stars, too. I would have to ask my dad to use some of his connections.

Jasmine and Sierra were having a heated discussion when I joined their table. I said, "Whatever you're arguing about now, squash it. I got some good news." Both set of eyes were on me. "I have three tickets to *High School Musical*."

"My mom tried to get tickets but was told it was sold out," Sierra said.

"You're going now. Isn't that great?"

Sierra and Jasmine were excited. We were talking over each other. Other kids were looking at our table to see what all the commotion was about. We were all in accord for the first time in months.

I found out from another student that we had a pop quiz in my sixth-hour class, so I had to cram for it during study hall. I knew I had an A in gym, because I'd passed all the levels of the physical test. I wasn't too sure what my grade would be for some of my other classes. They fluctuated up and down. My algebra class kicked my butt, so I would be lucky to get a B for the semester.

We checked our quiz papers before the class ended. I missed two, so I got eighty percent right. I could deal with a B. It only meant I had to study harder and get an A on the final exam. My main focus was on class, so I didn't immediately realize Marcus was walking right by me.

"Can a brother get a hug?" he asked.

I stopped walking. I moved my books from one arm to the other. "There are plenty of girls who would be willing to give you a hug."

"But I want one from you."

"Marcus, I don't have time. My mom's waiting for me."

"Bri, I'm not giving up."

I threw my hand up in the air and left to go find my mom.

~ 42 ~

A Change is Coming

Ms. Pearl's batch of chocolate chip cookies melted in my mouth. I ate over half a dozen as I sat at the kitchen table reading my history book. "You're going to spoil your dinner," Ms. Pearl said.

"I can't help it. These are so good." I reached for another one. She hit my hand. "Ouch."

"No more until after dinner."

"Yes, ma'am."

Ms. Pearl helped me with my homework by asking me a few questions. I went over the questions I kept missing. By the time she finished quizzing me, dinner was ready. My mom waddled to the table. My dad sat at the end of the table with his Blackberry in front of him and the Bluetooth glued to his ear. My mom frowned until he hung up the phone.

"Can't you give it a rest for at least thirty minutes?" she asked him.

"Destiny, now's not the time."

They went back and forth for a few minutes. Ms. Pearl and I looked at each other as I helped her place the food on the table. Ms. Pearl left and I took a seat. I could feel the tension.

My dad ignored my mom's rants and turned his attention toward me. "How's Marcus?"

That set my mom off again and she said, "If you took time out to spend with your daughter, you would know she and Marcus aren't seeing each other anymore."

"I was talking to Britney."

My mom threw her napkin on the table and pushed herself away as quick as she could in her condition. The scene was sort of hilarious, but I wouldn't dare laugh. "I'll be eating upstairs." She grabbed a roll, took a bite out of it, and placed it on her plate of food. She waddled out of the dining room. My dad looked at me. "I guess I better go make this right."

"You better, or we'll all have to suffer," I said, piling food on my plate.

Ms. Pearl came back into the room. "Those two are something else. They'll be fine. Her hormones are just getting the best of her."

"I hope so. Sometimes I don't know what to say to her because I don't know what mood she's going to be in."

"Having babies at her age isn't a piece of cake."

"I wished she wasn't having any, period," I said.

Ms. Pearl took a seat at the table. "Look here, Missy. You know I don't like getting in your family business." I stopped eating and looked at her. *Yeah, right.* Ms. Pearl never had a problem telling me how she felt about anything whether I asked for her opinion or not. I listened to her lecture me about my mom and the babies. "She needs all the support she can get, and the selfish way you've been acting worries me."

Good thing I had eaten those cookies earlier, because I was losing my appetite. "I support my mom," I said in my defense.

"I don't ever hear you asking her how she's doing. When she talks about the babies, the expression on your face says you could care less."

I didn't realize it was that obvious. "I can't help how I feel."

"You should be glad that you'll have siblings."

Since she wanted to be all up in our family business, I was going to let her know exactly how I felt. "I'm used to being the only child. I don't know how to share."

"You share with your friends all the time. Sharing with a little sister or brother will be a piece of cake."

"High school is supposed to be the best time of my life. I'm not going to have time to babysit."

"Your parents can afford a nanny, so I doubt if you'll do too much babysitting."

She had a comeback to every obstacle I mentioned. I doubted if she had a response to this one. "I'm used to being the center of my parents' eyes. Once the babies come, they won't even realize I'm here."

Ms. Pearl laughed. I didn't see anything funny. "Silly girl. Is that all you're worried about?" If she wanted a response from me, she wasn't getting it. She continued to say, "Your parents love you. You're their first. Nobody ever forgets the first. The first always holds a special place in their parents' hearts. These babies aren't meant to replace you."

I thought about what she said. I wanted life the way it used to be. With two kids on the way, I knew it would never be the same. My freshman year of high school seemed to be full of changes. I would do my best to be happy about the babies, but I couldn't make any solid promises.

My mom and dad were hugged up together on their bed. I could hear an old Sam Cooke song blasting from their speakers, "A Change is Going to Come."

The song fit perfectly for our life.

~ 43 ~

The Light

"Guess who I saw outside school yesterday?" Jasmine asked.

I didn't feel like playing the guessing game. "I don't know."

"Tanisha. Girl, she's gotten big."

"I guess she was up here to see her baby's daddy."

"Yep. And you should have seen how Sierra acted like the proud stepmama. She wouldn't leave DJ's side."

"Did you hear what they were talking about?"

"Now, you know me."

"I know, that's why I'm asking."

"DJ told her he wasn't doing anything until she had a blood test."

"She threatened to tell his parents."

"He called her all kinds of names."

"And Sierra just stood there?"

"Yep. Like a statue."

"Shhh. Here she comes."

Sierra walked up to where we stood. "What's up y'all?" she asked.

"Nothing much," I responded.

Jasmine wouldn't look in her direction. Sierra asked, "Can I borrow your science class notes?"

"I can make you a copy, but I'm not through studying," I said.

"So what's up with you and DJ?" Jasmine asked.

"I don't think that's any of your business."

We kept walking toward homeroom. "Looks like everybody was in your business yesterday."

"Let's stand over here," I said, as I led them to the area behind the door of our homeroom. That way we wouldn't be in clear view of our teacher. The tardy bell hadn't rung, so we still had some time.

"Tanisha is lying," Sierra said. "As soon as she has the baby, you and everybody else will see that."

I wanted to shake Sierra. When it came to DJ, she was so stupid. I hoped I never got that stupid over a boy. It was obvious to everybody but her that DJ was a jerk. Even Jasmine finally had opened up her eyes and left the jerk alone.

After gym, I decided to walk the long route to

class. As I was nearing a corner, I overheard two familiar voices. I stopped, and peeped around the corner to confirm who it was. DJ and Marcus. I eavesdropped on their conversation.

Marcus said, "Sierra's a good girl. Don't do it."

"Man, that girl will do anything I want. I'm going to be her first and make sure she never forgets it. And you know what they say about being the first." He started laughing.

Marcus laughed. *The jerk.* "But Sierra's a nice girl. After you sleep with her, then what?"

"There's too much of me to commit to one girl. Cheryl, Tanisha's friend, she's been trying to get with me. I'll probably give her a try next."

"Man, you're a dog."

DJ growled. "And you know it."

I released my breath, and turned to walk the other way to class. I had to warn Sierra. If she slept with DJ, she would not only lose her virginity to a jerk, but her heart would be broken because he planned on dumping her to be with someone else. I barely made it to my next class before the tardy bell rang.

After school, I rushed to find Sierra. Jasmine tapped me on my shoulder. "Why are you staring at Sierra and DJ?"

"Huh?"

She waved her hand in front of my eyes several

times. I blinked. "I need to talk to her." I repeated to Jasmine what I heard.

"Oh my goodness. I know Sierra and I haven't been getting along lately but there's no way I'm going to let that dude hurt my friend."

Jasmine walked in their direction. I rushed and stood in front of her to stop her. "No. Not here. He would only lie his way out of it."

"We have to warn her."

"I agree. But not like this."

"We need to get her by herself."

"From what I overheard it's supposed to happen this weekend."

"Let's go to the movies Friday and invite her. We can talk to her then."

"Good idea. I'll call her later."

Jasmine and I went our separate ways. I stood and watched Sierra and DJ as my mom pulled through the circular driveway. DJ had a smug look now, but not for long.

~ 44 ~

Just Say No

"She agreed to the movies." I informed Jasmine of the short conversation I'd had earlier that evening with Sierra.

"Brenda said she would drop us off and pick us up," she responded.

"Good. Until Friday, let's try to keep our mouths shut."

"It's going to be hard, because she's always talking about DJ this or DJ that."

"Now you see how I used to feel when you were doing that too."

"I was such a dummy."

I agreed, but didn't say it. "I got to go. That's Travis."

"Travis and Britney sitting in a tree," she sang.

I didn't listen to her finish. I clicked over. "How's it going?" he asked.

Travis wouldn't give up. He still gave me cute little cards at church, and text messages just to check on me. He had a way of making me feel special. I just didn't want to commit to him. If I was being real with myself, I had to admit a part of me still liked Marcus. More than Travis probably, but I did like Travis.

It seemed all of my teachers wanted to give quizzes before our big exams that would be in another week. I aced them all, except one. I would have gotten an A on it, but I missed the question about evolution. I considered telling my mom about it because from what I was taught, humans didn't evolve from apes, we evolved from Adam and Eve.

"You ready to get your weekend started?" Jasmine said, as she broke me out of my thoughts with her high-pitched voice.

I grabbed my backpack and walked outside with her to wait on Brenda. "Have you seen Sierra?" I asked.

"She's coming. I ran into her in the hallway. There's Brenda. Let me go stall her." I followed her to the car.

Brenda and I spoke. She pulled down her visor and applied some lipstick. "You girls better hurry up. I might have a date tonight and I need to get my nails done."

I looked down at her hands. Her nails looked freshly done. Jasmine left to go get Sierra. I got in the back of her car. The top was up because it was too cold to be riding with the top down. "I hear you girls are going to do an intervention," she said while looking at me in the rearview mirror.

"I hope it works."

She turned around in her seat. "Out of the three of you, you seem to be the one who thinks more logically. Don't let Jasmine do the talking."

"You know how your sister is."

"She thinks she knows everything, but she's got a lot to learn."

"Are y'all talking about me?" Jasmine asked. She opened up the door and Sierra got in the back.

"There's more to talk about in life than you," Brenda said, as she winked at me before turning back around and putting on her seat belt. "Buckle up girls, because I'm in a hurry."

Brenda didn't waste time getting us to the movie theater. We were barely out the car before she sped away. "I guess she was in a hurry," Sierra commented.

"She got to go get her nails done before it gets too crowded," Jasmine responded as we walked up to the window to buy our tickets.

We moved to the side because it took us a few minutes to agree on what we wanted to watch. We were limited to watching something PG-13 because we didn't have an adult to buy our tickets. We all agreed on the movie with Raven. I had an ulterior motive for choosing it: Raven's movies always made me laugh, and I wanted Sierra to be relaxed when we spoke to her about DJ.

The movie didn't disappoint. My side hurt from laughing so much. We went to the food court located near the movie theater and ordered burgers and fries. Jasmine ordered a veggie burger. It looked like ours but not as greasy.

Jasmine kept looking at me for a signal. We were halfway through eating when I said, "Sierra, I need to tell you something, but promise you won't get mad."

She wiped her mouth with her napkin. "If it's about DJ, I don't want to hear it."

Jasmine said, "Hear her out first."

Sierra folded her arms and leaned back in the chair. She got on the defensive without giving me a chance to tell her. I attempted to tell her in a calm voice what I had overheard. "If you go out with him tomorrow, he is going to make a move and he doesn't plan on taking no for an answer."

"DJ understands that I plan on being a virgin at least until after I graduate," she responded.

"The way he was talking to Marcus, it was like you

guys had planned a romantic date or something," I went on to say.

"Are you sure it was DJ talking? It could have been someone else Marcus was talking to."

"I know DJ's voice when I hear it. Besides, I saw him with my own two eyes."

"He probably knew you were there and that's why he said all those things."

Jasmine stopped eating. "Bri is only trying to save you from heartache, so listen to her."

"You two don't have boyfriends and you're just jealous."

I laughed. "Jealous of what? DJ's a playa, and I don't know about you, but me, I want a boy who has eyes only for me. Not me and every other hot girl."

"Exactly," Jasmine said. She gulped down her drink.

"You're one to talk. You were after DJ until he finally told you he didn't want you."

Jasmine put her drink down. She wiped her mouth with her napkin and looked Sierra directly in the eye. "So that's the lie he told you. DJ tried to sleep with me. I turned him down. I refuse to lose my virtue to someone like him."

"What if I did want to sleep with him?" Sierra asked.

Jasmine responded, "Then you're the biggest fool I've ever known."

Sierra looked at her watch. "What time did your sister say she was picking us up?"

"I'll call her now." Jasmine removed her phone from her backpack and called Brenda. She flipped the phone closed. "She'll be here in about fifteen minutes."

"So what are you going to do?" I asked.

"Nothing. I'm still going out with him tomorrow night," Sierra responded.

I hoped and prayed I would never be that stupid over one guy. I had done my duty: I had let her know what he was up to. The rest was up to her. I prayed she made the right decision.

~ 45 ~

No More Tears

"Let's have a girls' day," my mom said over break-fast Saturday morning.

I did want a new outfit, so I was all for shopping. "Give me thirty minutes and I'll be ready."

"No need to. I'll have someone come in and give us facials, pedicures, and massages. The works."

Maybe I could get the outfit later. I tried not to look disappointed. "Can we go to the Galleria later?"

"Dear, I don't feel like walking too much. These babies are kicking my butt."

"You can just drop me off and come back later to pick me up."

"I'll think about it." She called a few people and less than two hours later we were enjoying our facials.

I forgot all about the mall. My body felt relaxed after the Swedish massage. All I wanted to do was go to my room and sleep. Instead of going to the mall, I surfed the Net and found a few outfits and shoes. I clicked on the "buy" button and printed off my receipt so I could give to my mom for her records. I loved having my own credit card.

My grandmother said I was spoiled and she was right. I wondered what would change once the babies arrived. I was doing better after the talk with Ms. Pearl. I started to make an honest effort, and acted excited whenever my mom talked about the babies. I even pretended to be thrilled to see the sonogram picture they showed everyone.

Tonight was Sierra's date night and I wondered if she had changed her mind about going. I dialed her cell phone number several times. She answered the third time. "I'm out with DJ, what do you want?" she snapped.

"Excuse me. I'll talk to you later." I hung up the phone. She tried calling me back, but I hit the button to send it to my voice mail. *She's on a date so why call me back.*

I spent Sunday with my dad and mom. My dad treated us to dinner and the movies. I had the greatest dad in the world. Sometimes I wished he could spend more time with me, but I understood he had to work to make money. My mom complained some-times, but she and I were both accustomed to living a certain lifestyle. Dad's job afforded us to be able to live it. I had been thinking lately of what kind of ca-reer I should aim for. Whatever I chose, it had to pay lots of money. I liked helping people, so maybe some kind of doctor.

I was daydreaming about being an adult when my cell phone rang, breaking me out of my trance. I looked at the display and saw Marcus's name pop up. I should have deleted him from my contact list. I an-swered. He stuttered, "Have you talked to your friend?"

"No. I've been hanging out with the folks."

"Call her. I think she needs you right now."

I sat straight up on the bed. "What happened?"

"You need to talk to her."

"Look, you called me, so spill it."

"DJ will kill me."

"I already know about how he was supposed to get Sierra to sleep with him."

"What?"

"Please. Don't act surprised. I over heard y'all the other day in the hallway."

"You should have said something."

"I said something to my girl but she didn't want to listen. So what is it that you know?"

"DJ said Sierra slept with him last night."

"I don't believe that. She wouldn't. We have a pact."

"I tried to talk him out of it."

My heart rate increased. "For the record, I heard you laughing when DJ was talking about it."

"If you heard everything then you know I'm telling the truth."

The situation that had happened a few months before pushed to the front of my mind. I snapped, "Oh, no you didn't. When I tried to tell you about DJ when he forced a kiss on me, you didn't want to hear it. Funny how things are reversed."

"Come on. Don't hold what DJ did against me. I like Sierra. She's cool and I never wanted her to get mixed up with my cuz."

"Too late now. Look, I got to go. I need to find out how my friend's doing." I ended the call without waiting for him to respond.

I dialed Sierra's cell phone number but didn't get an answer. I dialed her home number and her little brother answered the phone. "She's in her room, crying."

"Zion, put her on the phone."

I listened to a few muffled sounds. He came back on the line. "She said that she doesn't want to talk."

"Tell her she either comes to the phone or I'll be

over there." I looked at the clock on the wall. It was after eight and I knew my mom wasn't going to take me over there, but I tried.

"Sierra said she'll see you at school tomorrow."

I called Jasmine and told her everything Marcus had said. "I'm in shock," Jasmine said. "We had agreed to not have sex until we were married or at least out of high school."

"Sierra said herself she wasn't. If anything, he forced himself on her, but she has to let us know. If he did, he's going to pay for this." My phone beeped. "That's Sierra. I'll call you right back."

"Do a three-way."

~ 46 ~

Payback

I answered the phone. "Girl, are you okay?" I could hear her crying. She blew her nose. I held the phone away because it sounded a little gross. She came back on the line. "DJ . . . he . . ." That's all she got out before she started crying again.

"Hold on, let me get Jasmine on the line," I said. I clicked over and dialed Jasmine's number. "Jas, don't say anything. Let me do all the talking." She agreed and I connected us all on the three-way. "Sierra, calm down and tell us what happened."

"We went to his house. His parents were out of town. I didn't know that or else I wouldn't have gone."

"What else?"

"I let him kiss me. I let him touch me and then he tried to." She paused.

By now I was sitting on the edge of my bed. "Did you do it?" I asked.

"I'm getting to that part. A part of me wanted to, but then I kept hearing your voice, Jas, my mom's, my preacher's. Everybody was telling me not to do it. He started undressing me and I let him. When he started to undress himself, that's when I asked him a question."

"What?" Jasmine asked.

"I asked him if he loved me and you know what he said? He said he could be in love, but he wouldn't know for sure until after we slept together. Who did he think I was?"

I knew she didn't want a real answer to that question, because she had been acting like she was missing a brain when it concerned him. I continued to listen.

"I realized at that moment he didn't love me. I grabbed my clothes and put them back on. He begged and begged me to sleep with him, but I just couldn't. The first time I do it, I want it to be with a boy who loves me. I can't believe I almost fell for it. When I asked him to take me home, he refused. I had to take a cab. I would have called Jas, but after having called her for Brenda the last time, I was just too embarrassed."

A part of me felt sorry for Sierra, but I also wanted to say, *that's what you get for not listening to me months ago.* "You should have called us. My mom would have brought me over there."

"And have her tell my mom, who would tell my dad? I don't think so."

I hated to be the bearer of bad news, but I had information she needed. "Marcus called me and told me DJ told him you guys slept together. That's why I called."

"Well, he's lying."

"I'm just telling you what he told Marcus."

Jasmine didn't say much during the course of the conversation. We all stayed on for about thirty minutes before going to bed. I almost overslept the next morning. I barely beat my mom downstairs. She wasn't dressed. "Mom, I'm going to be late if you don't hurry up."

She dragged herself to the table. "Your dad's dropping you off this morning."

Her eyes were puffy. I was concerned. "Mom, are you going to be okay?"

She rubbed her stomach. "Yes. These twins are just acting up this morning. I don't feel like doing anything."

She might not have felt like driving me to school, but she didn't have a problem stuffing her face with food. The whole time we talked, she piled her plate with slices of bacon and several slices of toast.

"Baby girl, you ready to go?" my dad asked as he grabbed a bagel off the table.

I stopped in the foyer and applied some lip gloss. I smacked my lips and followed my dad to his SUV. He played some new music from one of his singers and we jammed all the way to school. I really liked the one where Bow Wow made a guest appearance on the track. I couldn't wait to tell Sierra and Jasmine about the song. They were sitting in our normal spot. Sierra looked up. Her eyes were swollen and I could see tears flowing down her face.

Before I could ask a question, Jasmine said, "DJ's telling everybody Sierra slept with him."

"What? He's lying. Wait until I see him."

"I already gave him a piece of my mind, believe that," Jasmine said.

I dropped my backpack on the ground and sat on the other side of Sierra. "Hold your head up. You didn't do anything wrong."

"Everybody thinks I'm a slut and I didn't even do anything." The tears wouldn't stop flowing from her eyes. Jasmine handed her some tissues.

"Oh he's gone too far now," I said. I grabbed my

backpack and stormed through the front door of the school with one mission in mind, and that was to find Dylan Johnson.

I saw him smiling and laughing with a group of guys. Marcus was right there in the mix. Marcus saw me walking in their direction. He said something to DJ. I was too far to hear what was said. I kept walking. I put my backpack down as I neared them. In my mind I was slapping DJ upside his head, but when I got close to him, I just said one word, "Payback."

I walked away, leaving him to wonder what I meant.

~ 47 ~

The Plan

Sierra was embarrassed, and didn't want to eat lunch in the cafeteria. She had been dealing with stares and gossip all morning. Jasmine finally convinced her that she didn't do anything wrong so she had nothing to be ashamed about. With her head held high, she followed us into the cafeteria.

DJ made a snide remark when we passed the table. We had already said we would ignore him no matter what. I think we all exhaled once we sat down at our normal table. I saw a few people pointing and staring. Sierra wouldn't look up. She concentrated on the food on the tray.

"I wish I would have listened to you," she said, looking in my direction.

I took a bite of my dry sandwich before throwing it

back on the plate. "I could rub it in, but I'm not. I think you're dealing with enough as is."

Jasmine said, "At least you came to your senses before you actually did it."

"Then the rumors would be true."

"See, that's the bright side. Those are false rumors so let them talk," I said, dipping my fries in ketchup.

"It's easier for you to say. Your name isn't being plastered on MySpace and Facebook."

A light bulb went off in my head. I had a plan; a plan that, if implemented correctly, could stop DJ from hurting me or my friends again. He needed a dose of his own medicine and I was just the one to give it to him. "Ladies, I have a plan."

After school, we piled up into Brenda's car and she took us to the electronics store. We bought a few items and split the cost among us. Brenda said, "What are you girls going to do with that stuff you bought?"

We looked from one to the other. Jasmine said, "It's for a class."

"And I was born yesterday," she responded as we walked to the car.

The car beeped twice indicating the alarm was off, and we got in. "I hope you don't get caught, because wiretapping is illegal."

"Bren, you need to mind your own business," Jasmine said.

"I just don't want you ending up in jail. I'm too pretty to visit you behind bars."

Sierra laughed. If it took Brenda getting on Jasmine's nerves to put a smile on my friend's face, I was all for it. I hoped they kept it up. Brenda and Jasmine went back and forth talking about each other. My side was hurting by the time Brenda dropped me off. The items we bought came with me.

Once I was in the privacy of my room, I removed the items from the bag and read the instructions on how to use them. Tomorrow would be the day DJ would regret ever crossing me or any of my friends.

I could barely sleep thinking about our plan. The next day was cold outside, but I wore a skirt uniform anyway, so it would be easier for me to hide the recorder. I placed the rose-shaped pendant on the right of my chest. I got up extra early so I could curl my hair and fix my makeup.

"You're looking awfully cute this morning," my mom said as we ran into each other in the hallway.

"I don't have on too much makeup, do I?"

She tilted my face so she could look at it from various angles. "Looks like I did it myself."

My mom dropped me off at school. I made a point

of walking slowly and twisted past DJ, Marcus, and their little crew. I conveniently dropped something on the ground near them and had to bend down to pick it up. Sierra and Jasmine sat on a bench near the front stairway.

"Looking good," Sierra said as she touched my curly hair.

"Those guys were looking at you like a piece of meat," Jasmine said.

I pretty much knew DJ's schedule, so I made it a point to run past him all day. Each time I caught him staring, he was practically drooling. I pretended I couldn't wait to use the restroom right before lunchtime, and left early so I could be near DJ's class. When the bell rang and he exited, I "accidentally" bumped into him, and the two books I was holding fell on the floor.

"Britney, did anyone ever tell you you have some pretty hair?" he asked.

"You just did."

I made sure my hand touched DJ's hand longer than it should have when he handed me my books. "Why don't I walk you to the cafeteria?"

"What about Sierra?" I asked.

"Uh, she won't be a problem."

"You sure? I know how she feels about you. I'm not trying to come between you two."

"I'm surprised she didn't tell you, but we sort of broke up."

I acted like I was surprised. "Did this happen before or after you two slept together?"

"About that . . . I sort of lied about that because she pissed me off."

"So you're saying she didn't sleep with you?"

"No, she got scared. I tried to hit it but she wouldn't give it up. But forget Sierra, how about you and I hook up."

By now we were around the corner from the cafeteria. "I would hook up with you, but I used to go with your cousin."

"I have to admit, I'm not used to getting his leftovers, but, girl, you're worth it. I'll take you over any of these other girls any day."

"DJ, I don't think so. I'm not like you. I don't stab my friends in the back."

"But . . . but . . ." he stuttered and ran up behind me. He stopped when he saw Marcus.

I waved at Marcus. "How you doing?" and kept on walking through the cafeteria door. Jasmine and Sierra were already seated. I couldn't stop smiling. I had enough on tape to help repair Sierra's rep, and also show Marcus how low-down his cousin really was.

"Operation was successful."

"So we don't have to go to plan B," Jasmine said, sounding disappointed.

"Shhh. We don't want anyone to overhear us," I said, as I placed the straw in my carton of chocolate milk. "Why go to plan B, when plan A worked?"

~ 48 ~

My Space

Sierra and I went over to Jasmine's house. Jasmine's nineteen-year-old cousin Keith met her at her place. He helped us piece together the video and audio I had gotten earlier of DJ. He fixed it up and loaded it to a fake account. A bulletin message was sent out to the same folks who had received the note from DJ about Sierra.

I logged on to my account to make sure it went across. I clicked on the bulletin and saw and heard DJ say he lied about Sierra. The other video was sent to Marcus for his eyes and ears only. He could hear his cousin make the moves on his ex-girl. He could no longer be in denial.

"Young ladies, I would hate to get on your bad side," Keith said as he logged off the computer.

Jasmine said, "Well, DJ brought it on himself. He played me and Sierra and had the nerve to step to Bri."

"Can't blame him for trying. That's just how we are. It's up to you girls to keep us in check."

We left with Keith so he could drop us off. Keith was smart and cute and a girl's dream. I'd had a crush on Keith since I was in sixth grade. Of course, I would never admit it to Jasmine, or Sierra for that matter. I hoped he would be available when I turned eighteen. If so, I was going to marry him.

"Well, Bri. You're home."

"Thanks, Keith, for everything. Why do guys say stuff and try to ruin girls' reputations?"

"All guys aren't like this guy. Find you one that will respect you. If he disrespects you, kick him to the curb."

"I wished more guys were like you."

He smiled and laughed. "Well, there's only one of me to go around." He pulled up in my driveway. "Good night, Bri. Keep your head in those books now."

He waited until I was in the house. I waved at him from the doorway. He waved back and pulled off. "Who was that?" my mom asked, startling me.

"Jasmine's cousin, Keith."

"How old is he?" she asked.

"He's a freshman in college."

"Don't make it a habit."

"Mom, he just dropped me off so you wouldn't have to come pick me up. If it would make you feel any better, he dropped off Sierra too." I moved past her and headed up the stairs.

"Don't be getting sassy with me. I might be getting too big to spank you but I can still throw."

"Mom, I'm too old for whoopings."

"Say that to me after I have the twins and we'll see."

I looked down at her and she had a smile on her face, so I knew she was joking. I studied some and then logged on to the computer. Several people had responded to the anonymous broadcast. Neither Marcus nor DJ had seen it yet, because there weren't any comments on the board from either one of them.

"Girl, folks are dogging DJ out on the boards," Sierra said as soon as she answered her phone.

"I know. I wonder if he'll show up tomorrow at school."

"He has to. We have finals starting tomorrow. If he don't, he can fail this semester."

Jasmine sent me an instant message. We sent messages back and forth while I talked to Sierra on the phone. My dad knocked on the door and entered. "I'm about to take your mom to the hospital. She's having stomach pains."

"Sierra, I have to go." I hung up with her. "I'm coming, too," I said.

"No. Ms. Pearl will be here shortly. I want you to stay and get some rest. Keep your phone charged up. I'll call you."

An hour before my mom had been fine. I couldn't understand what was going on. I helped my dad get her in his SUV. "Get back in the house and turn the alarm on," my mom said, sounding more concerned about me than about herself. "I love you, baby. Now do as I say."

"I love you too, Mama." I did as I was told. I didn't want to upset her. I wasn't happy about the twins, but I didn't want anything to happen to them. I said a quick prayer for my mom and their safety as I looked out the window and watched them leave for the hospital. It didn't take long for Ms. Pearl to come. She did her best to comfort me. I stayed up until I received a phone call from my dad. "She just had a bad case of heart burn." I let out a sigh of relief.

~ 49 ~

No Regrets

The next morning, we all slept late. After checking on my mom, my dad and I left for school. My dad wrote me an excuse for first period. It seemed like the janitor was busier than usual. I picked up a flier that flew in front of me. I glanced at it before putting it in the garbage.

The janitor said, "That'll sure teach him about lying." He took it and balled the paper up. Apparently DJ had pissed off other girls, because I knew Jasmine, Sierra, and I didn't have anything to do with the fliers.

I handed the teacher my excuse and slid in my seat. Jasmine passed me a note and my eyes bugged when I read it. I looked up and shook my head up and down. "Is there something you want to share with the class, Ms. Franklin and Ms. McNeil?"

"No, ma'am," I said.

"Then I suggest you two wait until after class to talk about whatever it is."

"Yes, Mrs. Johnson," Jasmine said.

After class, we talked. "Girl, he is pissed."

"Now he knows how it feels to be the subject of a nasty rumor."

Sierra tapped me on my arm. "Here he comes."

"I can handle him," I responded.

"Britney, I know it was you who posted that message," DJ said.

My hand flew up. "Whatever. You can't prove anything."

"Why did you do it? I've never done anything to you."

I laughed in his face. "Tell that to someone else." I didn't see Marcus nor any of the other guys who normally hung around DJ. I asked, "Where's your sidekicks?"

He ignored my question, but said, "Marcus is mad at me thanks to you."

"For the record, I didn't do anything. It was all you."

"Don't let me catch you by yourself," he said.

A chill went down my spine. "Y'all heard that didn't you. He threatened me."

He laughed. "You're not even worth it. I'm trying to get a scholarship and I won't let you or any other girl stop me."

The hall monitor walked over. "The tardy bell has rung, so keep it moving."

We walked one way and DJ went another. "You don't think he'll try to hurt you?" Sierra asked.

"He can try. If he do, he'll regret it."

Sierra said, "Maybe we shouldn't have done it."

Jasmine said, "Please. I have no regrets."

"Neither do I," I said. "He got exactly what he deserved."

I saw Marcus sitting on the benches in the gym before class. He looked to be in his own little world. I walked up to him. "Hey, stranger."

He barely looked up. "What's up, Bri?"

I placed my hand on his shoulder. "Just checking on you. I didn't see you at lunchtime."

"I'm fine. Just dealing with some family drama."

"Everything all right at home?" I asked.

"No, this mess with DJ. Because of him, I lost you." He looked up at me showing his big brown puppy dog eyes.

"Don't let it get you down. We can still be friends."

"I want more than friendship."

"Now is not the time."

"I'm patient."

"And I'll be around," I said. I left him on the benches and went to change into my gym clothes.

DJ caught up with me after school as I was leaving my last class. "I have to hand it to you. You're good."

"DJ, I don't know what you're talking about."

"You cleared your girl's name. I know earlier I told you to watch your back, but it looks like I need to be watching my back. I got my eye on you, girl," he said, pointing at me as he quickened his pace, leaving me to walk behind him.

He turned around and pointed at me again. His gesture made me feel creepy. My mom's message said I was to ride home with Brenda. I figured Jasmine would be waiting outside for me, but she was nowhere to be found. When I finally spotted Brenda, I knocked on the window of her convertible to get her attention. She rolled the window down and I informed her, "My mom said you were dropping me off."

"Nobody told me anything, but hop in."

I got in the backseat and we waited for Jasmine. Brenda started complaining about Jasmine being tardy. I turned up the volume on my iPod to tune her out. Brenda and Jasmine were always going at it. I wasn't in the mood to listen to them today.

~ 50 ~

Finals

Our mission with DJ had been accomplished, however, we had finals so we had to push the small victory to the back of our minds and concentrate on our classes. Mrs. Johnson had several essay questions on her test. I know I aced the multiple choice sections, but didn't feel too confident about my answers on the essay part. She was unpredictable, so all I could do was pray that I got a good grade on the test.

My head hurt by the time I finished taking my algebra test. Nothing we had gone over in class was on the test. I tried to apply the principles I had learned. It would be a hit or miss with that particular test.

"Ms. Franklin, I need to see you in my office," Mr. Reese said, before I could go into my last class.

All I thought about as I followed him to his office was that he found out we were behind DJ's recording. I stood several inches over him but you couldn't help but respect his authority. He opened up his office door. "Take a seat."

He left me in his office for ten minutes. I hadn't been that nervous since my mom told me she was having a baby. My eyes scanned the room. I wanted to look at the files he had on his desk, but I didn't want to get caught. He came back in the room with my dad. I looked at my dad to see if I could read his face. His facial expression didn't reveal to me how much trouble I was in. I thought about what I was going to tell them about the DJ situation.

"Britney, we're proud to say we want to skip you up a grade."

I had opened my mouth to defend my actions. I closed it when it registered that this was good news. It had nothing to do with DJ. *Skipping a grade. Wow. Do I want to do that?*

"I'm proud of you, baby," my dad said with a huge smile on his face.

The vice-principal handed my dad a package. "Everything you need to know about the program is here. If she does decide to stay in the ninth grade, we would like for her to take more accelerated courses. We want to make sure her classes are challenging her. It's been my experience that when we don't keep them challenged, their grades suffer."

All I thought about was that I wasn't getting punished for the Internet recordings. Cool. I listened as Mr. Reese went through some of the things in the pamphlet. I didn't have any more tests, so my dad checked me out of school.

"Do you want to skip to the next grade?" he asked. "I think you're old enough to make that decision on your own."

It was a big decision. I would be leaving behind my friends, just when we were trying to mend things. This first part of our freshman year had been rocky. "I'm not sure. Let's talk to Mom first. I want to, but I don't want to."

"We'll do whatever you decide."

So much pressure and I was only fourteen. I remembered a conversation I'd had with my grandmother. She'd said that whenever she had a difficult decision to make, she prayed about it. From the way things looked, I had a lot of praying to do.

I spent the weekend with my parents. My mom's stomach was getting bigger and bigger. I was told she was being put on bed rest. My dad made arrangements for us to have a driver at our disposal. Sierra and Jasmine would be jealous, but, hey, I deserved to have my own driver after all the drama my folks had put me through this past semester.

"Britney, this is our driver, Mr. Donovan," my dad said.

I shook his hand. He reminded me of the guy from *Driving Miss Daisy*. I wasn't sure if the new driver would work out. I was expecting someone a little younger. This guy looked like he was about forty or fifty. He handed me a card. "This is my contact information. If for some reason you have to leave school early, call one of these numbers." I glanced at the card and placed it in my backpack.

I ran back upstairs to say good-bye to my mom. "Let me know how he drives."

I hugged her. "Believe me, I will."

It felt nice going to school in the back of a Rolls-Royce. I felt like Cinderella all over again. When we pulled up in front of the school, Mr. Donovan got out and held my door open. Haters were looking me up and down. "I'll be ready at three o'clock," I said before walking away.

"Oh, no wonder you didn't call me this weekend. You've been too busy living the good life," Jasmine said.

"Isn't there enough hating going around?" I said as we walked to class.

"Sierra's still tripping, so talk to her."

"Will the drama ever end?" I faced Jasmine. "What now?"

"I don't know. I called her this weekend and she practically cussed me out. I thought we were cool. Thought the DJ stuff was all behind us, but she kept throwing it up in my face. You know I'm only going to give you so much time to get over your stuff, so I let her have it."

My head dropped. "Jas, please. I don't know if I want to hear any more."

"Well, somebody had to tell her about her weight. If she's not careful, her weight is going to get out of control. I'm not a man stealer. I can get any boy I want. I just needed her to know why DJ was after her. She got a big butt and big boobs and the brain she has in between here," she pointed to her head, "she barely used when she was with him."

"If you said all of that to me, I would have told your butt off too," I responded.

"You need to be able to take it if you're going to dish it out. Sierra can't take it. I'm just trying to build her up a backbone so the next guy won't be able to take advantage of her like DJ."

I didn't have the energy to try to convince Jasmine she was wrong. Just when I thought our friendship was back on track, this happened. This was my month for our slumber party. Friday, we were going to nip this in the bud. For now, I had other things to do. I had a test to take and other decisions to make. Jasmine was still talking when I walked away from her.

~ 51 ~

Secret Santa

Having Mr. Donovan at my beck and call made me the envy of my friends and other kids in my classes. Yesterday after school, he took me to the store so I could buy all of my Christmas presents. We were exchanging gifts in our homeroom class at school. Our parents were invited to come, but I knew mine wouldn't be there. My mom was on bed rest and my dad was too busy making deals.

My dad paid for us to have a catered breakfast, but the teacher was sworn to silence. As far as the other students knew, Mrs. Johnson treated us to breakfast. It was time to exchange gifts. I handed Renee her gift. I hoped she liked it. She was sort of quiet, so it was hard to pick something out to fit her personality.

I had gotten her something I would want myself. I went over the allowed amount, but I could afford it so it wasn't a big deal.

Renee removed the paper, and it made me feel good when her eyes brightened as she opened up the box filled with various flavors of lip gloss. She surprised me by giving me a hug. "Thank you. I don't know which one to use first."

"I like the cotton candy." I picked it up out the box and handed it to her.

"Britney, here's your gift."

My secret Santa was Fredrick, the cute boy who sat behind me. I opened it up and saw it was a white box that held a silver charm. It was cute. It was shaped like a tube of lipstick or lip gloss. "I love it," I said.

"You're always putting on lip gloss, so when I saw it, I knew it was perfect for you."

"Thanks. Can you hook it on for me?"

Fredrick seemed nervous as he clamped on the charm. I twirled my wrist around. "Thanks."

I walked over to where Sierra and Jasmine where and we showed each other our gifts. The rest of the day went by fast because most of the teachers were busy grading papers while they gave us busy work to pass the time. It was one of those days where we really could have stayed home. I guess they figured we would be out for the next two weeks, so we could afford to be bored one day.

"You got company." Jasmine pointed near my locker.

"I'll catch up with you later," I said to her. "What's up, Marcus?"

He pulled a gift out from behind his back. "I have something for you. I wasn't sure if I would see you over the break, so I wanted to give it to you now."

I placed the box in my backpack. "Thanks. I didn't get you anything, though."

"That's okay. I didn't expect you to."

Since DJ had been exposed, Marcus looked like he lost his best friend. I felt bad for him, but not bad enough to be his girlfriend again. I wasn't ready for that. "Marcus."

He stopped walking. I walked up to him and hugged him. "Thanks for the gift. Call me over the break."

His eyes twinkled. He walked away with his shoulders back instead of slumped. I got my personal items out of my locker and placed them in my backpack. Jasmine and Sierra were both waiting for me outside. "I'm ready. You could have gone to the car. Mr. Donovan don't bite," I said. They followed me to the car. "Mr. Donovan, these are my best friends, Jasmine and Sierra."

He opened up the door. "Nice to meet you, ladies."

We chatted about our day at school all the way home. The aroma of cinnamon met us when we walked through the door. "This is beautiful," Sierra said, as we walked through the door toward the living room.

When I'd left that morning the house hadn't been decorated. Now it was decorated with all sorts of Christmas decorations. The huge Christmas tree sat in the center of the room. There were gifts already under it. I hoped a few were for me. Ms. Pearl walked in behind us. "You girls hungry?"

"Yes, ma'am," Jasmine responded for all of us.

"Wash up, and I'll have your meal ready for you at the table in about fifteen minutes."

I went to my parents' room while they went to wash up. I knocked on the door a few times. "Mama, can I come in?"

She finally let me in. "How do you like the house?" she asked as we hugged.

"Everything looks good. Any of those gifts for me?" I asked, as I jumped on the bed. She held her stomach. "Sorry," I said.

"They might be. You have to ask Santa about that."

"Jas and Sierra wanted to come in but I didn't know if you felt like being bothered."

"They could have come in. I'll come see them before the night is out. So what are you girls getting into?"

"Wish me luck, because tonight will be the ultimate test of our friendship."

~ 52 ~

Friend or Foe

Ms. Pearl's mouth-watering chocolate chip cookies were a hit with Sierra and Jasmine. They were snacking on them while waiting on me to join them for dinner. We piled our plates with lasagna and salad.

"Can vegetarians eat beef?" I asked, already knowing the answer, but teasing Jasmine because she had more lasagna on her plate than we did.

"I told you I was just thinking about it, so don't go acting like I am one yet."

We laughed and ate. Afterward, we went to my room. "I have some new nail polish," I said.

I pulled out a case filled with nail polish in a variety of colors. "Let's give each other manicures," Sierra suggested.

Jasmine looked at her nails. "Fine, but I want Bri to do mine."

Sierra rolled her eyes. "If you want to look like a clown go right ahead."

"So what you're trying to say? Bri can't do nails?"

"Hello. I'm standing right here." I stood between them.

"Fine. Let Bri do your nails. I'll do my own," Sierra said. She picked a shade of pink from the case, and sat at my vanity table.

"That's the color I was going to pick. It matches my lip gloss," Jasmine said.

"You both can use it. Come on now, Jas. You tripping," I said.

"She always wants what I have," Sierra said, dipping a cotton ball in the polish remover.

Jasmine walked near the vanity area. "I bet you want say it to my face."

Sierra looked up into Jasmine's face and said slowly, "She always wants what I have."

I grabbed Jasmine's hand just as she was about to slap Sierra. Sierra jumped up from the table and knocked over the fingernail polish. She grabbed the tissue to clean it up. "See what you made me do."

"Enough," I yelled. Both of them looked in my direction.

My mom happened to pick this time to walk in the room. "You girls okay?"

"Yes, Ms. Destiny."

Jasmine and Sierra acted like they weren't arguing only a few minutes before. They each took turns hugging my mom, or at least tried to hug her because her stomach poked out so much it was hard to get their arms around her.

"I just came to say hi. You can get back to what you were doing."

I followed my mom out of the room and closed the door. "Mom, I don't know what to do. They keep going at it."

She touched my chest in the area of my heart. "Pull from here. I've seen you in action. I'm confident you can make things right."

Too bad I wasn't so confident. I opened the door and both were still standing with their arms folded. "Sierra, you sit right here." I patted to one side of my bed. I walked around and patted on the other end of the bed. "Jas, you sit right here."

They folded their arms and their faces were frowned, but they obeyed. "Bri, you need to give it up," Jas said as she took a seat.

I shook my finger. "Nobody is allowed to talk right now but me." I looked back and forth between the two. "When we started our freshman year we were as close as three friends can be, but someone tried to drive a wedge between us."

"That's not my fault," Sierra said.

"I'm not placing blame on anyone; however we are all responsible." They looked at me, confused. "I was wrong for not listening to you all about your infatuation with DJ. I should have been more aggressive in showing you how he was no good to us individually or as a group." I looked at Sierra. "You temporarily turned your back on us. You lashed out at us because you were trying to hold on to a boy who only wanted to use you."

"See, that's what I've been saying all along," Jasmine added.

"And you. You knew Sierra liked DJ, so you should have been the bigger person and let her go after him. If she got hurt in the process, then that would have been on her. We are never *ever* to compete for the same boy."

"But . . . but," Jasmine stuttered.

"But nothing. DJ was almost the end of us, but I was determined not to let that happen. I don't want to take all of the credit for us still being friends. The bond, although fractured, is still there. That's what's kept us friends."

I sat on the bed between them. "We had final

exams this week. I don't know if we passed or failed. But we almost failed the ultimate test: that boys may come and go, but a best friend is forever."

Sierra started sniffling. "I'm sorry, y'all." She reached for my arm and I hugged her.

We looked at Jasmine. She tried not to give in to her feelings but she couldn't resist her two best friends giving her pitiful looks. "I'm sorry too. Can you ever forgive me?"

We hugged each other. "Bri, I want Sierra to do my manicure. She does do a better job than you."

"Whatever. I didn't want to do your ugly nails anyway."

Jasmine looked at her nails. "Please. You wish yours were this long."

I waited for Sierra to finish Jasmine's nail, so she could do mine. I picked up the latest fashion magazine. I folded the edges of the pages so I could find them easier later.

It was almost like old times; except we'd learned a valuable lesson: to never put a boy before your friends.

THE END